ASCENDED

Book Three of the Manipulated Series

By Harper North

Contents:

CHAPTER 1

THERE'S NO WAY THIS IS HAPPENING.

Dust swirls around our feet. The sun blazes hot over our heads and sweat trickles down my face as I stare into Lacy's cold, empty eyes.

"Lacy!" I scream, everything in me wanting to run to Drape. But her face remains lifeless. It's like every part of who she once was has been stolen and replaced by EHC commands. Not once does she glance down to Drape's body, lying limp at her feet. She's not the best friend I've known since we were kids.

She's a monster.

My heart beats rapid fire, and I run a hand through my hair as I try to figure out a way to get through to her. "You don't have to do this."

Her stare bores into me. "You don't get to tell me what to do."

Elias places his hand on my arm. His face is strained. He knows it's useless to try and bring back some ounce of her humanity, but I have to try.

"Maybe not." I gulp down my fear. "But Drape is your friend—he's *our* friend. *Not* the enemy."

I try to take a step forward, but a dozen guns raise in my direction. Elias grabs my arm and pulls me back. Emma glares, determination brimming over her face. Talen pulls back his shoulders like he's ready to die rather than be taken by them again. The EHC soldiers aren't going to make this easy. Just beyond them, a hovercraft waits on the ground. Another floats in the air, heat venting from its rotor blades. There has to be a way out of this.

Lacy smirks. "Don't even think about it."

"Just let us check on him," Emma says in her best reassuring voice.

"I don't think so," Lacy growls.

My veins tingle with the adrenaline streaming through them. Bouncing my attention from Drape to Lacy, I wipe the sweat from my forehead, quickly analyzing the position of the EHC operatives. They're scattered in V-formation in front of us. If the others from our group were still alive, maybe we could take them on, but without them, there's no way we can get out safely. Every escape route is blocked and we're heavily outnumbered. All the scenarios I run through in my mind show immediate death. For all of us.

Lacy tosses Drape onto his back like he's an empty sack. Her strong muscles bulge beneath the dark, fitted, Aura operative suit, every stitch designed to enhance her movement.

"If you care so much for your friend, I suggest you listen closely. Drape's alive for now, but soon…"

Relief fills me. That's something. I open my mouth to speak. To remind her who she is again. Who we are.

Lacy cuts me off. "You have *one* choice if you want to help your friend. That's the best deal you're going to get, trust me."

The weight of the situation bears down on me. So many people have died—Jase, Davis, Knuckles—it's almost too much.

"No," I say, refusing to accept that. "Talen was brought back, and you can be, too. It's not too late."

Her steely eyes remain fixed on me. It's like she wants me to make a move, just so she can tear me apart.

Okay. New tactic, because the old one's not working.

"What's going to happen to us?" I demand.

Lacy shifts her gaze to Talen. "Talen will be reconditioned and once again serve the EHC."

Talen winces. Despite his warrior's stance, broad shoulders, and that he towers a good foot over me, there's something vulnerable in him. He was so close to being free. He takes a moment to scan our surroundings as if he's also trying to figure a way out. He shakes his head, shoulders dropping as a blankness washes over his face.

"Lacy, he doesn't want to go back," I say. "None of us are going back."

A smooth, deep voice sounds from behind the twelve operatives. "That's not really up to you anymore, is it?"

There's something calming in the voice, but beside me, Elias digs his fingers into my arm. "Stop speaking," he hisses into my ear.

My eyes flick to the lanky man stepping out from behind the soldiers. Several red stripes run across the shoulder of his armored EHC uniform. The man, who must be in his late fifties, strides toward us without hesitation.

I lean into Elias. "Who's that?"

"He's an EHC commander," he mutters. "Now shut up."

"Yes, I am a commander," the man says, obviously having heard my question. "I'm Commander Reinhart. You've caused quite a disturbance," he continues as he scans over us, furrowing his brow. He turns to Lacy. "Thank you for your service."

Lacy nods and steps back, the perfect Aura operative, obedient to every order.

My gaze shifts to Drape and my throat tightens. His body is limp but for the shallow lifting and falling of his chest.

"I don't suggest you do anything foolish," Reinhart says, as if he knows what I might do next even before I know.

"He won't be alive much longer. He needs help," Emma insists, her eyes fixed on Reinhart.

A slow smile spreads across his face. "That could be arranged if you agree to come with us without causing any further problems."

I shake my head and swallow back my anger. "Everyone here knows that's not going to happen."

As the sun beats down on us, Reinhart looks me over, head to toe. The heartless look nearly sucks the air from my lungs.

Reinhart folds his hands behind his back and walks closer to Elias, ignoring my words. "Your uprising has created some problems for us."

"I hope so," Elias replies, raising his chin.

Reinhart presses his lips into a thin line. "You won't be saying that shortly."

"Why wouldn't I?"

"Rebels have always existed, but they haven't always succeeded."

"We succeeded. We made the broadcast," Emma says, facing the commander.

Reinhart spins around and leans closer to her. "Do you truly believe that you are the first rebel group who has tried to do something like this?"

Emma maintains her firm stance. "Things will never be the same, though."

My chest swells with pride. Even if these are our last few moments on Earth, at least we did something to stand up to the corruption and cruelty of a broken government.

The commander holds his gaze on Emma for a moment then turns and walks around our group, examining each of us. The hairs on the back of my neck stiffen when he nears me.

"Your attempt to overthrow the EHC created a media and public crisis," he says to no one in particular. "You are correct in that assumption."

He lingers in front of me for a moment, then turns back toward Elias, eyeing him.

"You were a Noble class citizen…" he narrows his eyes, "…a privileged class citizen who defected and aided Dwellers in an uprising. Disappointing."

Elias pulls his shoulders back and lifts his chin even higher.

Next, Reinhart turns toward Emma. "And you are the granddaughter of EHC co-founder Edward Nejem, yet you threw it all away when you ran away and illegally housed people with natural immunity. A pity to be born with such great potential."

Emma's green eyes spark. "I'm not afraid of you."

A sly grin spreads across the commander's face. "You will be."

I straighten as nerves consume me.

"Someone had to help those people," she says dryly.

"Meddling in government affairs will cost you—more than you can afford." Reinhart shifts his attention toward Talen. "Defective property of the EHC that aided known terrorists."

Talen's glare hardens, a scowl tightening his chiseled jawline.

The commander makes his way back to the front of our group. To me. "Finley A298. Illegally modified Noble class who... sparked a revolution."

"So, you know who we are," I mutter.

"I've known who you are for some time now," he says, placing his hands behind his back. "And I know of the others who helped your rebellion. In fact, the EHC knows of every rebel who attempts to overthrow the government. Sky Breslin, for example. A friend of yours, right?"

My chest aches at the mention of Sky's name.

"A scavenger from an underground Slack network."

"Where is he?" I demand.

Reinhart's brow lifts. "You care?"

"Is he alive?"

"Mr. Breslin is being processed in Ethos."

"Processed?" Does that mean he's dead or alive?

The commander removes a cloth from his pocket and dabs the sweat from his face. "He is being processed for his upcoming trial."

"Trial?" I shake my head. "The EHC has no legitimate legal system, only tyranny."

"Nevertheless, there will be a trial," the commander says.

"And what about us?" Emma interjects. "Will we stand trial, too?"

Reinhart neatly folds the cloth. "There are two choices for you," he says, tucking the cloth back into his pocket. "You can try and escape," he turns to look at me, "but you *will* be caught, one way or another. The operatives will shoot you, or Lacy could do much worse."

Lacy grins as she sets her eyes on me.

"Or, you can stand trial."

"For what?" I challenge, fully knowing that our actions are in direct opposition to the EHC. "We did nothing but help the people who worked so hard to—"

"War crimes," Reinhart says.

My voice catches in my throat.

"So, if you're done with this little rebellion of yours and are ready to surrender, the operatives will take you to the hovercraft. You will be brought to Ethos to stand trial, just like your friend Sky, for crimes against the EHC."

I shake my head as I try to imagine a desperate escape, but there's no hope of that. Surrender is our only choice—for now.

CHAPTER 2

"LET GO OF ME!"

I twist back and forth, trying to get away from a burly op that's twice my size. He must be Century class. His steely gaze burns with hatred.

I could claw his eyes out or punch him in the gut and make a run for it. My mind runs through the calculations one more time—it's no use. The twenty operatives will take me down, or worse, and Lacy will have me wrangled and back on the hovercraft within seconds.

The op nails my ribcage with his gun and pain zigzags up my side.

"Okay... o—" I start to say when he flips me over. My face smacks the ground and the air rips from my lungs.

Elias shouts something that might be, "*Get off of her!*" but it's all muffled beneath the dull ringing in my ears. The operative's knee wrenches against my back. He's fumbling with something. I gasp for air. My lungs burn like fire. Black spots float in front of my eyes. I try to shift away from him, but the guard digs his knee in harder as he secures something around my wrists.

"Stop fighting," the operative hisses in my ear, "or I'm gonna make this worse for you."

I relent, the taste of earth and iron filling my mouth. He slowly releases his knee. The air rushes back into my lungs. A second later, I'm on my feet.

"Get them into the hovercraft!" Commander Reinhart orders.

Elias yanks away violently as another operative drags him toward the hovercraft. There's a look of concern on Elias' face as he strains his neck to check on me.

I'm fine.

I lift my chin and grit my teeth as the operative shoves me toward the hovercraft. I turn to face him. "Get your hands off me," I growl and spit the blood and dirt in my mouth to the ground. The op smirks.

I scan the area for Drape. He's gone, and my throat tightens as my thoughts tease me with horrible outcomes. To my left are Emma and Talen. Emma's face is tight with anger as Lacy clamps cuffs around her wrists.

"You don't have to do this," Emma says to Lacy.

Lacy narrows her eyes and grins. There's something in the expression that turns my stomach. She's relishing in the opportunity to take us in, but a part of me knows she wants more. The power coursing through her body is corrupting her.

Lacy ignores Emma. She nods to an operative that leads her away, and then turns toward a broken Talen, cuffing him in a flash. He doesn't even try to fight her.

Little good that'll do. I chuckle to myself. A set of cuffs is nothing. Talen can drop these fools to the ground in...

Before I can finish the thought, the ops carry out a metallic device and secure it around his neck. They seal it with a quick flick of a button, and Talen groans as the device squeezes around his throat. I'm sure this device is a bit more sophisticated than the one Emma fashioned from spare parts.

The commander sneers. "We don't want you using the abilities we so graciously gave you, now, do we?"

We're ushered inside the hovercraft and into some kind of cargo hold. *I thought I'd never have to see another one of these.* A stifling, metallic smell in the air mixes with the heat from outside and makes me want to gag. Dozens of containers and tech gear that I can't identify surround us.

Within minutes, the operatives have us secured into chairs. Elias and Talen sit across from Emma and me. At least they're keeping us together—all of us except Drape. I shift around, pulling at my restraint to see if he's behind us. The operatives hover nearby just in case we plan on rebelling again. Already my mind is calculating the possibilities of escape in this scenario. They're still low. Actually, they're zero. Armed guards, cuffed wrists, a body running on little food or water—there's no chance, and they know it, too.

"Where's Drape?" I demand, looking at the nearest op. None of them even look at me.

A low murmur below my feet grabs my attention, then a sudden shift of the hovercraft makes my chest tighten. Seconds later, we're airborne.

I narrow my gaze at the op standing at my side, the same one who put me on the ground. "Can't you tell me if he's even alive?"

He slowly turns his head toward me. "Med-bay," he says, returning his fixed gaze to an empty mark on the opposite wall. "Now shut your mouth."

"He'd better be okay," I warn, ignoring him.

"Drape is Century class," Emma says, pulling my attention back to her. "He's strong. He'll make it."

I try to relax my stiff body, but it's impossible due to the ache in my back from the operative's knee. Elias' eyes shift back and forth, probably trying to figure out a plan to get us out of here. Talen's eyes, on the other hand, are distant.

"What's going to happen to us?" I ask him.

With what little movement the restraint offers, Talen shakes his head, as if there's no hope for us once we arrive at Ethos.

I crane my neck to look at Emma. She presses her lips together. Her eyes flash to Elias and then the guards. I follow their non-verbal signals, trying to make sense of what's going on between them. After a moment, Emma says in a hushed voice, "The trial will be all for show."

Of course it will be, duh. The EHC is one big dog and pony show, and we're going to be the main act.

Elias takes a deep breath. "We have to hope that the others who heard our message will help us."

"The EHC will make it look like the message was meaningless," Emma whispers. "They'll want to regain order and show their might."

"Stop talking!" one of the ops snaps.

I chew on my lip. What's going on right now in Ethos, not to mention the rest of the world? The commander said our message caused problems, but how many people saw it? Maybe there's open rebellion in the city right now. I lean back hard in my chair and squeeze my eyes shut, imagining some EHC leader reading a list of our crimes before a fake jury. He'll spin everything to make it sound like we're terrorists and they're the good guys who have been unfairly attacked.

"You're going to have to be even stronger than before," Emma says.

I slowly open my eyes.

Another operative glares at her. The ops don't want us talking, but who are they to tell us what to do?

Across from me, Talen's eyes are heavy. He tries to take a breath, but the metal around his neck is tight against him. He leans his chin closer to his chest. "No matter how strong you are," he whispers, "the EHC will find a way to destroy you."

"They won't!" I shout, drawing a few of the operatives' attention. "You won't destroy us."

Two of them ignore me. One operative smirks like he's looking forward to getting the chance to prove me wrong. The gruff op who cuffed me steps closer and pulls back his fist like he's going to punch me in the gut.

Elias tries to stand, but an operative shoves him back down. "Don't even—"

Pain sears into my cheek as the operative lands a firm punch. My teeth rattle and my head throbs. I taste coppery blood inside my mouth again.

"Stop it!" Emma orders.

I shake my head and try to refocus while twisting at my cuffs. Three movements to reach for his gun. Two movements to subdue the operative. One movement to put a bullet in his head.

"You can't kill us," Talen says. "Reinhart needs his trial, remember?"

The op grimaces and slides back to the wall, but it's clear from the look on his face that this is far from over. I make sure to give him the same glare before I turn to Emma. "So how do we defend ourselves at the trial?"

Emma shakes her head. Her eyes flick to the operatives, then back to us. She lowers her voice to barely a whisper and says, "We'll be limited in what we can say, how we can defend ourselves, and then—"

"We'll be sentenced to death," I finish for her.

Elias glares hard at me. "Keep it together. There might be a way to work around it."

"How?"

"A friend of Mason's had a trial in Ethos. It was a joke. Set Mason's efforts back for years. But it caused enough of a stir that they didn't kill him. Just discredited and locked him up."

I sit up in my chair. "That doesn't sound very promising."

"Keep it *down*," Emma hisses as her eyes flick to the guards.

My shoulders drop, and I lean back again. My arms ache and the cuffs dig into my wrists. A dull, aching pain works its way into my neck. I try to rotate my jaw. I have to distract myself from this.

"You okay?" I ask Talen. *Of course he's not okay.*

He raises his chin. "I *won't* become an Aura op again. I'd rather die." He glares at the men surrounding us. "Following orders like good dogs?" he taunts them. *"Woof, woof!"*

"Stop it." Emma leans closer. "We can't jeopardize everything now."

"They're good dogs," Talen says. "Stay! Don't move! Good boys!"

A slow smile works its way across my face. With each one of his taunts, I feel somewhat compensated for what just happened.

Elias starts to smile, too. He opens his mouth to join in when Emma shoots him a serious scowl.

"Don't do it," she warns.

"Why not?" Elias asks. "Talen's right. They have to give us our fake trial. They're not going to kill us on this hovercraft."

She swallows and takes a deep breath, turning back to Talen. "You have to bide your time."

Talen shakes his head. "There's not much of that left."

"Your ability is only limited by the restraint," she says. "At some point they'll have to remove it."

"I had my chance," Talen sighs. "And it didn't work. I don't care if I die anymore."

My eyes widen. "Wait," I say to him. "Emma's right. You can still fight. There might be another chance if you don't lose hope."

Talen's face tightens as he shakes his head back and forth.

"You *still* have a family out there," I insist in a hushed breath.

Bang. The sound from behind us makes me jump and twist around. Two operatives drag Drape across the floor through an open hatch. My heart skips a beat. Drape's eyes flutter open and then close. He groans as they toss him into a chair beside us.

I wait a full three seconds after the ops leave before I start bombarding Drape with questions. "Drape, can you hear me?"

"Keep it down!" one of the ops growls.

"Or what?" I snap back.

He marches toward me again, the same guy who cuffed me earlier. This guy sure likes to pick on me. It's okay, I can take whatever he doles out.

"Let her check on her friend," Emma pleads in a soothing tone.

Elias glances up at the man. "You don't want to be responsible for killing another one of us, do you? Think how bad that'll look at the trial."

I wait for the guard to say no, but instead he comes over to me and takes the cuffs off my wrists.

"You have one minute," he says.

There's still time to kill him. Three moves. But if I take him, the rest of them will be on top of me and I won't be able to check on Drape. Right now, Drape is more important. I rub my wrists and then scoot to Drape's side.

"Can you hear me?" I ask again.

Drape groans and shifts in his chair. Finally, his eyelids drift open. His gaze shifts around the room and then lands on me. He brings a hand to his forehead. "Fin?"

"We thought we lost you," I say, smoothing back his hair. There's a nasty cut peeking out of his hairline and a few bruises on his face to match.

"Lacy," Drape whispers.

"Forget her," Elias says.

Drape places his hands in his lap. He stares at them for a second, then says, "I know what she is. I saw her kill them. I saw—"

"Stop," Emma interrupts. "You don't have to tell us. We know—"

"She killed Knuckles and Jase."

"We know," I say, squatting down beside him.

Drape's soft eyes turn to me. "I tried to get her to stop, but she wouldn't listen."

I glance over to Elias. Deep wrinkles line his brow. "They were our friends," he says. "They didn't deserve to die, but the Lacy you knew is gone."

"He's right," Talen agrees. "The true Lacy is buried, trapped in her own body. All that's left is amplified aggression and loyalty for the EHC."

I rock back on my heels, remembering when Lacy hated the EHC and everything they stood for. She must be buried *really* deep.

"It's true for most Aura ops," Talen adds. "When we're first programmed, all we want to do is fight and feel the power. Lacy is blinded by it."

"There's no way for her to come back like this," Elias says.

I quickly jump up. "She can. If anyone can, it's Lacy. She'll use the same strength she's always had to fight her way back."

"No way," Elias shoots back. "After killing Jase and Knuckles? There's no way Lacy could come back and live with herself for that."

The hovercraft rumbles again, the vibrations slowing.

The operative latches onto my arm—almost tighter this time if that's possible—and puts the cuffs on me again. "Back to your seat."

I make sure to shoot him a death stare as he tosses me into my seat. Emma leans close to me. "When we arrive, follow my lead. We're not done yet." She turns to Talen, quirking a brow. "It's in *you* to make things right."

I glance toward Emma and then back to Talen. What does she mean by that? My mind flashes to when we took Talen captive. Emma reprogrammed him, broke through the EHC code, and brought Talen back to humanity.

She did something to Talen.

Talen's eyes shift back and forth. He sits up a little taller in his chair. A slow smile spreads across his face as he pulls his shoulders back.

Emma again leans closer to me, just as the hovercraft's vibrations stop and the whirling noise goes silent. "I *always* have a failsafe for my projects."

CHAPTER 3

"NO ONE MOVES!" the tall op nearest to me snarls. "We wait until we get our orders."

I struggle to breathe in a lungful of hot, thick air, raking over my already parched tongue and throat. How much longer?

Heavy boots clanking on the metal floor jar me back to my senses. Commander Reinhart marches into the cargo hold with Lacy tailing him. A smug grin stretches across her lips, and a large, silver pulse rifle is strapped across her chest. The combo sends a shiver down my spine.

Reinhart breezes straight past us to a button alongside the bay door and presses it. The action triggers a mechanical release. There's a *pop*, followed by the slow whirling sound of the massive back cargo hold door opening. I gasp as a gush of fresh, warm air circulates through the room. It's not great, but it's better than the stifling heat. I flick my attention outside. Rays of sunlight shine against the door, casting deep shadows—*late afternoon*.

More soldiers wait on the outside of the cargo door. No way can I take down the ops inside on my own. Even with Elias, Emma, and Talen, the possibility of making it out alive is low. Maybe fifteen percent. I chew on my lip.

"Get up!" an op orders.

In an instant, I'm on my feet.

My guard leans in closer. "Don't even try to fight, cause if you do," he hisses, "I'll be the first one to put a bullet in that pretty little head of yours."

"Get away from me," I snap as he seizes my arms and drags me toward the exit.

Behind me, two ops pull Talen to his feet and a third grabs Emma, bringing her to my side. I strain my neck to get a better view of outside, where I can make out several more hovercrafts and some large operational equipment.

"Welcome to Ethos," Commander Reinhart says to Elias in a superior tone.

Elias struggles with the operative restraining him. "How did we get here so fast?" he demands, twisting away.

Commander Reinhart's self-righteous smile shrinks to a stubborn line. He narrows his eyes as the operative fumbles to regain control of Elias. A second op intervenes, jabbing his gun against Elias' lower back. Elias winces and relents.

"Why are you trying to fight?" I snap in his direction. "You must've done the calculations, too."

"She's right," Reinhart says, glaring at Elias. "Escape is pointless. The transports are faster than citizen vehicles. You'll find that many things you believed about your capabilities are nothing compared to what the EHC is truly capable of."

There's something plastic about Reinhart, phony and irritating. Just his presence sends a shiver down my spine. He slowly turns and heads down the ramp with Lacy. The ops pull us behind, and I squint in the afternoon light.

Around us are dozens of hovercrafts and other military vehicles, lining an immense airbase. My chest tightens at the sight. There's more technology in this one base than I've seen in my entire life. On the hazy horizon are tall, sleek buildings with red lights flashing on their roofs, and transports on the ground zip after one another. Everything is structured, perfectly synchronized.

Underground, in the mines, we were covered in dirt most of the time and totally devoid of the advanced tech that pours out of every corner of this place. And it was all built on our backs. The corners of my eyes sting with angry tears as we're marched toward another hovercraft, this one smaller than the one we arrived in.

"Get in," an op orders us.

Talen reluctantly climbs up. Emma follows. Before the ops shove Elias inside, he turns to face me.

"I don't have any brilliant escape plans," he says, catching a glimpse of my expression.

I swallow and shake my head. He should have told me what Ethos would be like, but I wonder if he didn't in the hopes that I'd never have to feel the way I do right now.

The op shoves me from behind, flinging me into the vehicle in a heap. Drape's already inside, but barely conscious, propped up in the corner.

Lacy grins as she and Reinhart climb in last and sit in front of me.

"Where are you taking us?" Emma demands.

Reinhart ignores her. There's no point in trying to get anything out of him.

The transport shifts and again we're moving, but the ride is so smooth you might not even know it if you weren't paying attention. The air in the cabin is clean and filtered, the seats comfortable. Unable to bring myself to look at Lacy again, I turn my gaze through the long windows. Outside are more transports and a larger terminal that I'm sure we'll never see the inside of. Not the likes of us. Criminals and the citizens of Ethos will never interact.

As the transport glides right, we're suddenly out of the operations base and entering the city. My eyes widen as I try to take in my surroundings, mind bouncing, processing the new sights. The transport weaves around other vehicles seamlessly. Towering above us are the buildings I spotted from the landing site. Up close, they're even more spectacular. Glass windows reflect images of transporters and a city full of movement. The pathways are unnaturally lined with bright green grass and towering trees between the buildings and roadways. Hovercrafts zip and zag above us with perfect precision. On the walkways below, well-dressed citizens mill around, their clothes nothing like our worn shirts and bland, functional cargo pants. Everything about this city is modern.

A pit forms in my stomach. Underground, we went days with little food, doing hard labor using equipment that sometimes worked, but more often failed. Angry tears well up in my eyes again as I bite down on my lip, refusing to let Reinhart see me like this.

"You never stood a chance," Reinhart says, drawing my attention away from the window.

I release a slow breath, then raise my eyes to him. "How can you treat the Dwellers so badly? They're given so little—"

"You may find it surprising to know I have family underground," Reinhart says.

My heart clenches. *"What?"*

Reinhart lowers his gaze. "Everyone has a place in this world. It's not personal. Each person serves an important function in maintaining life on a radically changing Earth."

"You've got to be kidding," Elias spits.

Reinhart shifts to face him. "If the underground system was to fail, so would society, and no one would survive."

Elias leans forward, determination filling his eyes. "A unified population would create harmony and the collective efforts would adapt to the Earth much faster."

"Our studies and projections show a much different picture," Reinhart says flatly.

"A suppressed people will only lead to constant conflict!" Elias argues.

"That is why we have a legal system. To maintain order."

Emma raises a brow. "I was part of this society before and witnessed over and over again the potential of humanity buried in order to maintain power."

Reinhart scoffs. "You've been away for too long to understand the ways of a successful society."

"So much effort is used to keep the privileged in power," Emma says. "The progress of Ethos has been slowed. Everyone is on the brink of extinction."

"Look around," Reinhart says, pointing to the towers in the distance. "Does it look like we are on the brink of extinction?"

"All your studies are skewed to your advantage, you're just too blind to see it!" Elias shouts.

Reinhart's jaw clenches. Lacy tightens her grip on her gun, but I'm not ready to back down.

"One more uprising and there won't be any more Ethos," I say.

Lacy is on her feet in a flash and lunging for me. In one quick motion, she shoves her gun into my chest, her other hand reaching out to me. A pit forms in my stomach at the thought of feeling another Aura attack.

Without flinching, I stare hard into her dark eyes, almost inviting her to kill me. Reinhart clears his throat, pulling Lacy's attention away. She returns to her seat, leaving me with my heart crashing into my ribcage.

Talen shifts himself to glare at Lacy. He shakes his head at what must be a reflection of his former self.

Reinhart leans back in his seat and folds his arms across his chest. "Stomping out rebellions is just an everyday task for the EHC. It's no more of a hassle than stopping common theft."

Emma opens her mouth to speak, and Reinhart raises his hand to stay her. "Your little rebellion was pathetic. Where did it get you?"

No one answers.

"All the death and loss you went through," Reinhart sighs, "and for what? A simple media spin and quick trial. Everything you've done only helps our effort to eliminate uprisings even faster and more quietly than before."

"No," I say, blocking out his attempt at brainwashing.

As the commander opens his mouth, probably to spit more insults, a crackling sound from the cockpit interrupts him.

"We're arriving at Command," the disembodied voice says.

I gaze out the window again. The landscape has shifted while Reinhart was insulting us. The transport glides smoothly up the side of a massive skyscraper. Within moments, we land on top of the building. The Commander opens the door, and again the ops drag us out of the transport. Drape is on his feet now, but the way his eyelids keep drooping shut I'm pretty sure he could pass out again at any second.

"Take them to Bellaton," Reinhart commands, then looks straight at me. "Lacy and I will meet up with you later."

My mind spins as I study our surroundings. Outside of the transporter, the warm wind blows my hair in every direction, ripping through my flimsy clothes. We're led through a side door and into a building. Inside, I'm hit with cool air, and goosebumps form on my arms. Must be artificial climate control. We're forced down several flights of stairs and in another few moments we're taken to an open area in the heart of the building.

"Take a seat," the guard behind me barks to all of us, shoving me toward a series of tan, fabric covered chairs.

I obey and lower myself into it. *Whoa.* The soft fabric and cushion gives beneath me. If I weren't about to die, or whatever, this would be about as close to heaven as it gets. The ceilings stretch up fifty or so feet above, with ornate light fixtures hanging from smooth white tiling. A wall of glass surrounds us, and lush trees line the edge. The polished ground sparkles so cleanly I can see my reflection, which is not sparkling or clean. My hair is a tangled mess, desperate for a good wash. To avoid dwelling on that, I turn my gaze to the moving staircases that spiral upwards, carrying citizens to every corner of the building.

The ops hover a little too close, as if they're worried we might interact with some of the people, especially Talen, whose size and physique stands out from the rest of us.

From across the room, a woman wearing a grey, stylish suit emerges from a side room. Head held high, she's tall and slender, mid-forties, with medium-length blonde hair. She walks straight toward us. When she finally reaches us, she smiles, revealing a row of perfect, white teeth.

"Hello," she greets us. "My name is Director Flora Bellaton."

Elias sneers in her direction.

"Director of what? The EHC?" Emma demands.

Bellaton shoots Emma a don't-mess-with-me glare. "Correct. Get them up," she orders the ops, who promptly bring us to our feet. She then turns a cold stare on us. "Follow me, please."

Bellaton is the head of the EHC. She's the one that shapes every aspect of our lives from behind the walls of this glass tower.

The director leads us back through the atrium to a smaller room with large floor-to-ceiling windows. Outside, a crack of sunlight settles over the city, but the floor lights illuminate the space. A long metal table and several chairs fill the room. My attention goes immediately to the dozen or so glasses of water in the center of the table.

"Sit," Bellaton says, holding out her hand.

No need to tell me twice. I race for a chair at the far end and grab a glass of water, downing it. Emma, Jase, Drape, and Talen do the same. The coolness of the chilled water coats my throat as it goes down. I hold back an exhilarated sigh, not wanting them to see how much I enjoyed that, but I'm sure they already know.

Bellaton sits down across from me. "Take another," she offers.

I don't resist and grab a second, quickly drinking half of it.

"I understand your frustration," she continues.

"Really?" I wipe a drip of water from my chin with the back of my hand.

"Your human nature drives you to do what you do. The problem is that human nature is flawed."

I examine Bellaton's flawless face. I bet there's not a flaw in her at all, inside or out. "You want me to be less *human*?"

She folds her hands on the table. "We tried to weed out the defects in your genetics."

"*My* genetics?"

Bellaton raises a brow. She's all business now. "Not yours, per se, but your kind. There's an innate desire in the lower class to strive for more."

"By more," I lean in, "do you mean equality?"

"Humanity has already established a hierarchy." She leans back. "We have to protect what we have earned."

Hate burns in my core for this woman. "What's your plan for us?"

"If dwellers cannot be tamed, you will be erased and made an example of."

Talen pounds his fist on the table, face tight with anger. "Taming people and turning them into your personal pets is *not* how humanity works. I've lived in your system and I want nothing to do with it."

A slow smile spreads across Bellaton's face. "Take him."

"Take him?" I cry out. "Where?"

The ops surround Talen and pull him out of his chair.

"Leave him alone!" I shout.

Elias leaps up, but an op shoves him back down into his chair. Emma's face is calm, as if she's already prepared for all of this to happen.

As the ops drag Talen to the doorway, Bellaton slowly stands. "You have already been tamed once," she says to him. "All you need is an upgrade and you will be the asset the EHC needs to protect our way of life again."

My mouth drops open.

"You'll never succeed," Talen says with confidence.

Bellaton ignores him and waves her hand at the air. "Get him out of here."

"You should take him more seriously," Emma warns.

I watch Talen, expecting rage or fear to be consuming him, but instead, with a sly grin, his determined eyes meet mine.

He's got other plans.

CHAPTER 4

MY EYE CATCHES Emma's. A wry smile broadens across her face, and my mind races through what she could have programmed Talen with. A secret skill of sorts, I'm sure, but what? Can he break through that neck brace? Take on three guards at once? Maybe he's had the capability this whole time, but if he did, then why didn't he use it before we were dragged in front of Bellaton?

"I knew your mother," Emma says, interrupting my thoughts.

Emma stares at Bellaton now. There's a calm, all-knowing look in Emma's eyes.

Bellaton lifts her chin. "Did you?"

"She worked at the same research facility as I did. I was a bit younger than her. She was a good person, almost like a mentor."

Bellaton narrows her eyes. I press my back into my chair, enjoying the show.

"Do you think she would be proud of you?" Emma asks.

My chest tightens as the two women glare at one another. I take another gulp of water and glance to Elias, whose hands are folded in his lap.

Bellaton crosses her legs as a smirk stretches across her lips. "Your trial will begin as soon as possible. First, there will be a public announcement of the accused."

"Don't leave out any details." I laugh. "Make sure you broadcast to all of Ethos that you caught the criminals who dared to threaten your phony empire."

Without missing a beat, Bellaton shifts her gaze to Drape. It's like I don't even exist. "This is where the EHC states the crimes to the people and announces the trial."

"A perfect way to steer public opinion," Elias says.

She waves his comment away. "Next, you will be assigned a Combatant Defender."

There's a twinge in my gut at the mention of us being made to look like the combatants when we weren't the ones who started this.

"You will have twenty-four hours to plan your defense, and then the trial begins."

"A closed trial, right?" Emma asks.

Bellaton nods. "The trial will be closed."

"Convenient," Emma sighs.

"After that, the verdict will be read to the public."

There's no use in listening to her talk. I already know what a performance this whole thing is. Nothing good will come of it. I swivel my chair closer to Drape. His face is pale. I pour him a glass of water. He takes it and sips the liquid.

"Why bother with the trial?" I ask, shooting Bellaton a dark glare of my own. "Why not just say it all happened the way you want to spin it and be done with it?"

"We have certain procedures to be followed." She straightens her jacket. "Without them, society fails to function."

"Your system is broken," I say.

She slowly pushes back from the table. "There's no use in arguing. This is the procedure." She stands and turns toward the guards. "Take them to be processed, then straight to the holding center."

"Is that it?" I yell, jumping out of my seat. "Why'd you bring us here if you're not even going to consider what we said?"

"There's no use," Elias says to me. "Don't waste your breath."

As Bellaton leaves the room, the guards surround us.

"I'm *going*," I snap as one of the guards pulls on my arm a little too hard.

I follow Emma and Elias, making sure to help Drape along. We're taken across a walkway that connects us to the building next door. Never once do we have to step outside. How convenient of them to make sure we don't mingle with the rest of the population.

We pass through double doors, and the moment we step foot off the walkway and into the second building the air-controlled temperature disappears. Blocks of cemented walls separate one room from the next. A dim yellow light clings to everything in the windowless space. Blank brown walls jut up against a sterile white ceiling. My body tightens the farther we go, and I turn back to see the doors have closed behind us. *No going back.*

Up ahead, a female op waits. "Clean clothes." She hands me a folded shirt, pants, and a towel, then points toward a room across the hall. "You get five minutes to shower."

Shower?

I head into the small room and close the door. An automatic light flicks on overhead. There's no window or chance of escape here, so I peel off my grimy old clothes and kick them into the corner. I flick on the nozzle and wait for warm water, but it never comes. A cold shower it is. I jump in and scrub my hair and body with the soap from a dispenser on the wall. Probably from the shock of the freezing water on my skin, my mind is suddenly jolted full of energy and thoughts. I want to figure a way out, but a part of me knows if I do, I'll only interfere with Emma's plans.

I twist the nozzle off and towel off. After, I change into the fitted dark pants and a basic blue tank top.

My breath hitches as the door flies open.

"Time's up," the same guard who gave me the clothes orders. She grabs the towel from my hand.

With my hair still dripping wet, I'm led down another hall and into a room with stark, white light. I squint and hold my hand to my eyes to block it. As my vision adjusts, I can see Emma, Elias, and Drape in fresh clothes on a long bench set against a wall. I quickly find a seat next to them. Wet spots soak through the fabric of their similar, plain clothing. Emma's wet hair is pulled back into a bun. Elias runs his fingers through his. Drape sits there staring into space, making me wonder if he's feeling any better. Before I can ask, a tray of food is dropped in front of each of us.

My eyes widen. My mouth waters. My stomach wakens. It's been too long since our last meal. I reach down and grab the food, devouring fresh vegetables and fruit, as well as some sort of dark protein that is the most savory thing I've ever tried. We eat in silence, desperately refueling our malnourished bodies. Elias and Emma eat steadily. Drape is slower but manages to take small bites from his food. A part of me wonders if these guards even know how bad we had it underground. A shower and fresh food like this is a luxury.

And they call this prison.

"One minute," the guard shouts out as we chow down on the last of what's offered. Before I can finish the last bite, I'm dragged to my feet again.

"What's the rush?" I ask. "It's not like we're getting out of here anytime soon."

The stone-faced guard doesn't respond to my question. Instead, he marches me down the hallway toward a room filled with glass holding cells. That has to be the prison wing. Up ahead, I can make out the silhouette of someone inside one of the small cells, but I can't make out their features.

I gulp back worry. *What if there are real criminals locked up here?*

As we get closer, my heart picks up speed as a familiar outline begins to take shape. My eyes lock with Sky's. His lips form a tentative smile, and I'm nearly knocking down the guards to get closer, but my awareness of their Tenant class strength keeps me in place—for now.

"Hold still," one of them orders. He unlocks a cell next to Sky's and shoves me inside. Thick glass walls surround me, and a stark white wall is at my back.

Sky's eyes fill with life, but his body is thinner than I remember. He quickly moves to the glass surface and places a hand on the wall between us. He doesn't say a word.

I press up to the glass in my cell. "Are you alright?" I ask.

He taps on the glass and shakes his head. I realize sound is not able to escape the thick walls. All this time of being unsure how he is, and with him now just feet away, I can't even speak to him.

The guard leads Emma, Elias, and Drape inside their own personal cells. Elias nods to Sky. Drape manages a grin and Sky returns the gesture, concern filling his face.

I gnaw on my lip and scan my surroundings. A basic bench jutting from the bright white backing is all that we have. I feel like I'm an animal on display.

Sky presses both palms on the glass beside me. I do the same. Seeing that Sky is alive brings me some comfort, and my mind is flooded with the memories of when I saw him last. Our conversation. The kiss. If only we had more time. If only the ops didn't descend on Emma's camp and destroy everything.

I try to examine Sky more closely, hoping he wasn't tortured. I want to signal to him in some way, try to form some kind of communication system. I clench my fists and spin around, frustrated. It's so unfair.

On the other side of my glass prison, Elias is sitting on his own white bench. His eyes are focused on me and his lips are pressed together as if he's reading my mind about Sky.

I pace back and forth in my tiny cell. I have to figure a way to get out of here. Waiting for Talen or Emma's plan is taking too much time. My chest tightens as if fifty percent of the oxygen were sucked from my cell. I yank at my tank top and gasp for a deep breath. I need more air into my lungs.

My mind relives the path we used to get here. Past the dining area, showers, and changing rooms, processing, down a long walkway, and back through the first building toward the exit. I can do it. I can get out of here. There are eight guards surrounding us, another dozen or so on the way out, a security camera at every corner and doorway…

No, it's a low chance of all of us escaping. I run the calculations again. Five percent bounces back to me, and that's only because of unpredictable EHC op factors I'm not aware of.

I drop down onto the bench and lean my head against the glass. Five percent isn't enough. Reinhart was right—their advancements are more sophisticated, more evolved, than what I have.

But I still have my enhancement. I can still try.

I stand, go to the door, and use all of my strength, hoping to force it open. Sweat trickles down my forehead, rolling to my cheeks and chin. I blow out a sharp breath. The door won't budge. Figures they got a door to hold Noble class people. I glance back to Sky and then Elias. Both are sitting on their benches now. Guess the odds have been calculated. None of us are leaving.

Emma gives me a reassuring look. Drape smiles. Something in his expression makes me feel hopeful.

I return to the bench and try to figure out how I'm going to make it over the next few days when the trial begins to take shape. The crowds will hear of our rebellion. They will form their opinions and we'll be whisked away to face death. It won't even bother the citizens of Ethos that the judgment could be wrong. They'll say, *Even if it's wrong, why would we question the EHC?* To them, life is perfect. They know little of the underground struggle, and if they do, they probably put it out of their minds most of the time. Our broadcast has most likely been twisted so many ways that it's just irrelevant noise. Technology improves every day. The world is full of opportunity, but they don't know what's coming. The citizens don't know they're only moments away from catastrophe. Their way of life is so fragile.

Beyond my cell, three armed ops enter the main area connecting our joined cells. Just as they walk toward the center of the room, they violently stiffen before dropping to the ground, their faces filled with agony.

I know an Aura attack when I see one.

Talen.

I jump up and press my forehead against the glass. Elias, Emma, Drape, and Sky do the same.

"*Hurry,*" I whisper, desperate to get out of here.

Talen rushes in with his hand raised and a determined glare on his face.

The guards' faces contort, and they tear at their throats. Their mouths hang open, and I can only imagine hearing the gut-wrenching screams that are echoing off the prison walls. A second later, all three ops stop convulsing and become lifeless.

Beside me, Elias nods and mouths, *It's time.*

CHAPTER 5

I POUND MY fists against the cell wall, but only a dull echo comes back to me.

I dart my eyes to the door, and then back to the lifeless bodies of the three guards. The lights flicker overhead. A door off to the side automatically swings open, then shuts. This is our only chance to escape. I press my forehead to the glass, watching as the whole room seems to be malfunctioning.

In one swift move, Talen moves toward one of the dead bodies and rifles through the man's pocket, pulling out a key device. I swallow back my nerves as Talen presses a few buttons on the small device. Suddenly, all of the cell doors open with a *pop*. I release a long-held breath and rush from my cell to Sky.

"Are you all right?" I ask, throwing my arms around him. I pull back and search his eyes for an honest answer.

"I'm fine," he says. His gaze is fixed on Talen. "What was that?"

"He's an Aura op," I say. "Well, he was."

Sky takes a step back from the door. His shoulders stiffen. "A *what* op?"

"Don't worry. He's with us. I'll explain later." I inch closer and reach out my hand to him. "Are you sure you're okay?"

A wry smile spreads across his face as his eyes go to my hand. He reaches out and grabs hold of it. "I should have known once you guys arrived I'd be a free man again."

"Did you ever doubt us?"

He steps closer. "Not for a moment."

"Talen!" Emma calls.

I turn in time to see Elias shaking Talen's hand and Emma smiling. It's by far the biggest grin I've ever seen on her face.

"Come on," I say to Sky and start toward the others. In the cell beside us, Drape stands in the doorway. I wave for him to follow, stepping carefully over one of the guard's bodies. The man's twisted, red face reminds me of what an Aura op is truly capable of. *A horrible death.* I shiver and force myself to look away, trying not to remember my own near-death experience.

"Sky!" Elias slaps his shoulder. "Good to see you again."

"A friend of yours?" Talen asks.

"Talen," I say, "this is Sky. He was captured at Emma's camp. He's been helping us since the beginning."

Talen nods hello, but Sky is fixed to his spot. He opens his mouth to say something—

"We don't have much time," Emma interrupts. "Someone needs to get Drape out of his cell."

What?

I spin around to find Drape now sitting on the bench inside his cell, clearly in a daze.

"What's wrong with him?" Sky asks.

There isn't time to fill him in on how our supposed friend Lacy pummeled Drape in the desert, nearly killing him.

"He's hurt," I say instead. "Come on. Let's get him out of there."

The moment I step inside Drape's cell, my insides feel like they might come unglued. Nothing could be worse than getting locked in again. "Drape," I urge, "we have to leave."

He doesn't respond, so I step closer to where he sits on the bench. His knees are drawn to his chin.

I reach out a hand and place it on his shoulder. Still, Drape doesn't budge. Soft, muffled sobs come from him as I sit beside him. "We don't have much time," I whisper. "If we don't go now, we may not get another chance."

"It doesn't matter," Drape moans. "No matter what we do, nothing will change."

"That's not true," Sky says.

Drape raises his head. Tears spill down his cheeks. My chest tightens at the sight of his brokenness. I lock eyes with him. "You don't have to be strong right now. You just have to come."

He nods and wipes his face, then turns his gaze to Sky. "You finally decide to join us again?"

Sky stares, baffled. I choke back a laugh. One minute tears, the next jokes.

"So?" Drape asks.

"EHC interrogation and solitary confinement," Sky says. "I guess it helped that we didn't have a plan before I was taken. I didn't have anything new to tell them. They brought me up here yesterday." He looks around the cell. "I can't even tell you how good it is to see your faces again."

My heart pounds at his words. A small glint of hope in Sky's eyes reflects back to me.

"Let's get out of here," Drape says, standing and disrupting whatever connection is slowly rebuilding between Sky and me.

We head outside the cell to where Emma and Elias are collecting the guards' pulse weapons.

"My programming worked," Emma says, holstering one of the guns.

Elias shoves a pistol into his waistband and swivels back to face Emma. "How'd you do it?"

"I hid a little virus that would shut down the reprogramming process and disable their network."

"The *whole* network?" I ask, realizing the genius in Emma's work.

She nods and goes to a desk station beside the cells and rummages through the drawers.

"Like a charm," Talen says. "Sent the whole reprogramming Center into chaos mode. Once that happened, I easily broke free and—"

"We have to go," Elias interrupts. "There may be chaos, but they'll be here soon."

Emma slams one of the drawers shut. She tosses me a gun and waves for us to follow.

"What's our plan?" I ask as Elias kicks open the double doors ahead of us.

"Survive," Emma replies.

I glance back to Drape. "Stay close."

He nods. His face is flushed, and there's a weakness to each one of his steps, but he keeps up as we head back through the long corridors toward Building One. Whatever Lacy did to him must have temporarily weakened his modification.

The moment we cross over the walkway, several ops take aim at our group. Talen raises a hand, easily taking out two of the men at the end of the hallway. Several Ethos citizens scream and duck beneath tables or hide behind chairs. With a few sharp hits from my elbow and an uppercut from Elias, we manage to subdue several ops who rush toward us. They're down before they even have time to fire their weapons.

"Down this way!" I shout to Sky and Drape, remembering the long spiraling staircases and the exits from when we were first brought in.

I descend the staircase with the others following. A few more ops race up the stairs toward me. I raise my gun and fire a few rounds. They back away, but that won't last long. I glance over the railing and calculate the chance of survival if I drop down to the ground. It's not an easy jump, but it's doable, so before the ops have a chance to return fire, I turn to Sky and Drape and wave for them to follow. Then I leap the twelve or so feet to the ground, landing with a *thud*, but staying on my feet.

Seeing me crouched in front of them sends several more people screaming and rushing out the front door of the building. A moment later, Sky lands at my side. I glance up just in time to see Drape take a leap and tumble to the ground, rolling to soften the blow. Elias, Emma, and Talen blast their way through the ops on the staircase, taking them out and racing down.

My heart pounds as adrenaline pumps through my veins. We're out the doors a few seconds later. It's night—the sky above is dark, but the city is alive with light and people. Breathing heavily, I try to take it all in, absorb my surroundings in case we're ever back here again, but there's little time. A high-pitched, blaring sound blasts throughout the city streets. Sides of buildings that only seconds before were glass windows are now showing our faces.

My profile is plastered on a street sign. Drape's appears on a shop display. Elias' face is blown up to a twelve-foot hologram only feet away from where we stand. The words, *"Terrorist. Escape. Armed. Dangerous."* flash beneath each one of our images. A few people scream out as they spot us and rush from the street into the safety of the nearby shops.

"There's a back alley over there!" Talen shouts.

I swallow and chase after him, heading into the dark, narrow passage.

"I know a place where we can hide," Emma says between breaths, but how in the world are we ever going to be able to hide with our face being broadcast everywhere?

My feet pound the pavement. My lungs feel strong, but my head is a jumbled maze of calculations and possibility as I try to determine who or what might jump out in front of us. I need to figure out if this is the best way to go, or if we're just heading straight toward another trap.

At the end of the alley is another group of fancily-dressed people. They're all reading handheld devices and talking until one of them looks up and sees our group running straight toward them. The woman holding her device quickly presses several buttons. My mind jumps to what she's probably typing.

"They know where we are!" I shout.

"We can't worry about that," Elias says.

Emma steers us toward another alley and then through a series of winding corridors until we're far away from any main area where people might see us. She cranes her neck in all directions.

"Up there," she says, looking up at a towering structure. "My cousin lives in this apartment complex."

"Are you sure?" I ask as we stop in front of a glass door that leads into the building.

Emma takes a deep breath. "I've kept in contact with him for years. I never wanted to put him in danger, but what choice do we have?"

"You sure we can trust him?" Elias asks, running a hand through his hair.

Nodding, Emma says, "He's a low-level Transportation officer. He won't raise any red flags with the EHC."

Elias shoves the door open and we go inside. We follow him into a stairwell, and Emma leads us up three flights to a long hall with steel grey doors lining the wall, each spaced apart by a few yards. Pointing up, she counts down the numbers above the doors until she stops at the one labeled '311'. She raps on the door. A moment later, it opens.

A man that looks like he could be Emma's twin stands there wide-eyed for a moment, then quickly ushers our group inside.

"I'm sorry, Karim," Emma says to her cousin once we're all in.

He leads us toward a sitting area. "I haven't seen you in years, Emma." He wraps his arms around her shoulders. She returns the embrace.

I sit and take long, slow breaths as I survey the apartment and Emma's cousin. His dark skin and determined gaze match Emma's. The room is simple. A basic hologram player flashes our images in front of us. Karim releases Emma and moves toward the image and waves a hand. It vanishes, but not before showing our group running down the alley.

"There are cameras everywhere," Talen says. "It won't be long before they'll track us down."

Emma sighs. "Either that, or they'll check our potential family connections."

Elias turns to Sky. "You alright?"

"I'm fine," Sky says, still out of breath. "Thanks for keeping Fin safe."

Elias nods. "More like she's kept *us* safe."

Sky sits forward. "Hey, where's Lacy? And Jase and the others?"

"It's just us now," Elias says, avoiding eye contact with any of us.

Sky's eyes widen. "They're dead?"

"Not all of them," I say, turning my gaze down. "Lacy's with the EHC now. They turned her into a monster." I avoid looking at Talen.

"What?" Sky asks.

"She didn't have a choice." Talen looks out the window at the other end of the room. "Once they inject those nanos, you're not *you* anymore."

I stand and make my way across the room to him. "Thank you for coming back," I say. "You didn't have to stick around and save us."

"Of course I did," he replies, glancing back to me. "I meant it when I said I could never go back to the way I was. I don't want to be a *monster* anymore. I owe you for bringing me back."

"I didn't mean—"

"You're right," Talen cuts me off. "I *was* a monster. I hurt a lot of good people, and I have to live with that. But we have to bring the EHC down."

I nod, but again my mind spins through the ways to do so. Stuck in the middle of Ethos, the whole city either turned against us or afraid of us, with almost no supplies or help...

I dig my nails into my palms, refusing to feel hopeless. We've come too far.

Karim hands us each some fruit and crackers. "If I knew... I would have more to offer."

"It's okay," Emma says. Her face is tight, and she turns and paces the room. "This is fine." She takes an apple and eats it.

"My wife and daughter are gone for the day. But they have clothes you can wear," he says, pointing Emma and me to a room down the hall. He looks back toward the guys and then down at himself. "I'm shorter than any of you, but I think my shirts should work."

Emma nods her thanks.

He returns his attention to us. "Please, find whatever you need and take it. There are others like me who know the broadcast you sent out was true, no matter how the EHC tried to spin it."

"Thank you," I say, following Emma toward the back room. I rush to find a change of gray, slim fit pants, and a green shirt. I slip off my prison wear and put on his daughter's clothes, examining myself in the mirror. I look just like a citizen of Ethos now.

Emma does the same, choosing a black pair of pants and a simple button-down shirt. "We must go," she says, fastening the last button, urgency in her voice.

I follow her back out to the sitting area where the others wait, already changed. Each of them wears a new shirt, but the same pants we received back at the holding center.

Elias has a bag strapped across his chest and is loading it with the fruit and water bottles Karim offers. "There's no telling how long it will take for us to get out of Ethos."

"Is that the plan?" I ask.

There's determination in Elias' eyes. "We can get back to the desert, hide out, regroup. We'll find another way to fight."

Emma's eyes well with tears as she wraps her arms around her cousin. "Thank you," she whispers.

I pull back my shoulders and follow the others out of the apartment. Again, we head down the stairs and back out onto the street. It's dark and quiet, still early morning. Too quiet. My pulse picks up. My eyes dart to every corner of the alley and the top of every building as I try to stay alert.

We're only half a block away from Karim's building when a terrible blast rips through the air behind us. I cover my ears and turn back in time to see the dark smoke pouring from the apartment building. Piles of debris litter the ground. Screams echo through the alley, and the sound of gunfire follows.

Emma's eyes go wide. She covers her heart with one hand and cries out, but Elias pulls her away.

"It's too late," Elias says to her. "He's dead by now."

"No!" Emma sobs.

Drape turns her around and links arms with Emma, pulling her down the street and away from the chaos behind us.

My heart pounds in my chest. I stand rooted to the ground until Sky shakes my arm. "We have to go," he says, jarring me back to reality. "If they catch us down here, we'll be back in that cell in less than an hour and forget about a second chance at escaping."

I nod and let him guide me down the alley. We follow in Emma and Drape's footsteps. I shake free from Sky and chase after Elias and Talen, pulling out the weapon Emma gave me. I've had enough. I'm ready to use it again. I'm not going back to that cell. No one is going to stop us from helping the forgotten people underground—*my* people.

As we turn the corner, disappearing deeper into the city, a broadcast alert flashes overhead on a large digital display nearby. *Escaped terrorists*, it reads, again showing our faces one by one, *have now blown up a residential apartment, killing an EHC citizen.*

Karim's face shows on the screen, and my stomach drops as I realize what the EHC's strongest weapon is.

"Manipulation," I whisper, wondering how we'll ever fight something so powerful.

CHAPTER 6

"THIS WAY!" Elias shouts.

I'm nearly out of breath as we turn yet another corner through the winding maze of Ethos. Elias waves us toward what looks like the end of an alleyway. A brick wall that seems out of place in this high-tech setting looms ahead. Above us, the thrumming sound of hovercrafts echo in the near-dawn sky. Several waste receptacles line the two sides of the buildings that we stand between, and the air is thick with the smell of chemicals that will only get worse once the hot sun is up.

"Where are we?" Drape asks once we come to a stop.

I try to swallow, but my throat is dry, and the taste of dust lingers on my tongue. "What are you doing?" I ask Elias as he drops to the ground and pushes back dirt and other debris.

A siren wails behind us, followed by several loud shouts. *They're almost here.* My heart pounds as I turn back to see Emma kneeling on the ground beside Elias.

"It's still here," she says, choking back sobs.

I don't know what it is they're looking for, but I crouch down to help them. As we brush away more dirt, something rectangular and metallic appears.

"A little help, please." Emma gestures to Talen, and I move back to give him some space.

Talen bends down, and in one swift movement he rips open the covering, revealing a three-foot hole. A cool wind blows over all of us. Without saying a word, Elias shoves both of his legs into the hole. Half of his body disappears as he slowly descends a ladder into what looks like it might be an old sewer system.

"Come on," he orders.

Emma immediately follows.

My chest tightens, and I dart my attention to Sky and Drape. The sound of the siren nears. I shove my weapon in the back of my pants and with a trembling hand, I grab hold of the edges of the ladder and lower myself onto the first rung, then slowly, step by step, climb down into the dark, subterranean world.

A familiar but dank, musty smell sinks in. My hands grasp the cold metal of the ladder. I glance down, not knowing how far I'll have to climb. Already, Elias and Emma have disappeared. Following me, Drape and Sky are silhouetted by the soft glow of morning until Talen steps foot onto the ladder and slides the hatch above us shut.

Suddenly, I'm plunged into darkness. Only the sounds of the other's breathing are of some comfort now as I continue to lower myself. My mind travels back to the days of living underground. There's something reassuring in the dark, but also somehow terrifying at the same time.

My foot slips and I let out a scream.

"Fin!" Sky calls.

I find my footing. "I'm fine," I call back, comforted by his voice. This should be easy, but my nerves are getting the best of me.

"You're almost there," Elias says. His voice sounds close. I lower myself several steps until a dim light begins to give shape to the forms below. Emma's face is twenty feet beneath me. I sigh and take a deep breath, then descend the rungs, jumping down the last four or five feet.

Once I'm on solid ground, I scan the area. It's not a sewer at all. There's no waste or filthy water. Earthen smells mingle with the scent of sawdust and other building supplies.

Sky jumps down from the ladder, and we wait until Drape and Talen reach the bottom to join us.

"Where are we?" I ask, searching Elias' eyes.

"It's an old transit tunnel," explains says. "Most of the larger EHC cities have them. They were used before hover tech was implemented."

Without hesitating, Sky runs ahead.

"Where's he going?" Talen asks.

"To survey the tunnel, I'm sure," I say, remembering how Sky always took lead on scouting when we tried to make our way out of the Slack and old mining tunnels.

Emma, Talen, and Elias whisper together while Drape presses his back against the wall, catching his breath. I step next to the smooth wall and trace the perfectly constructed surface with my hand. The ten-foot-wide space is lit every few feet with a built-in lighting system. Some of the lights flicker, but it's enough to see up and down the long stretch of path. Everything the EHC builds is done with precision and confidence.

My breath hitches as I realize it won't be long before they figure out where we are. The cameras on the streets would have tracked our movements to the alley. I reach back into my waistband for the gun, cradling it between my hands and vowing never to let them take me back to that, or any other cell again.

Sky rushes back to our group. "There's an abandoned shaft up ahead."

"Excellent," Elias says. "We should hide out there."

"It's dark, though," Sky says. "It hasn't been completed."

"Perfect," Talen replies as he begins to move ahead. "Then it won't be on the EHC maps."

Emma nods her agreement. "It's our best chance for now."

We follow Sky down the dimly lit tunnel. I keep one hand on my gun and the other on the cold, hard surface of the tunnel wall until we get to the turn. Once there, my heart sinks. The unfinished tunnel is worse than Sky said. It's not just dark, it's pitch black. I strain my eyes as I try to make sense of where we're heading.

As if thinking the same thing, Talen says, "I can rewire the lights. Make a connection between the main tunnel and—"

"No," Emma stops him. "Then, they'll know where we are. They'll be on to us in no time."

"We can't travel in the dark," I argue.

She presses her lips together and turns to head back the way we came. Moments later, she returns with something in her hands.

I squint, trying to see what she's holding. "What's that?"

"A makeshift torch. I remember passing some old tunneling equipment back there. Those things are filled with machine grease. And this dirty rag and piece of rebar will work just fine."

She pulls out her pulse weapon and extends the torch in her other hand. A quick tap of the gun and a short burst of blue plasma ignites the grease, illuminating our surroundings.

Elias jumps into action gathering rags and loose pieces of metal from the ground. A few minutes later, we all have lit torches.

"Let's move," Elias says.

We start down the tunnel. Building supplies litter the floor. Occasional tools, scattered bolts and brackets, as well as wiring lay exposed every few feet.

I try to calculate how far this tunnel goes based on the length of the earlier tunnel shafts. Each one leads further down into the core of this underground system. After a few more minutes of walking, a scratchy cough works its way into my throat. I try to swallow, but my throat is still dry. Elias notices and tosses me a water bottle from his bag. Not wanting to waste it all, I take a small sip to sooth the scratch.

"Thanks," I say, tossing it back.

He nods and smiles.

"We should camp here," Emma suggests.

I nod, grateful for a break. I slide my gun back into my waistband. We prop up our torches around us.

"Let's get a fire going. These torches won't last long," Elias says, pointing to a pile of building planks in the corner.

Drape and Sky quickly gather the different sized planks while Talen and I dump out bags of nails and begin to tear apart the paper to make kindling. Elias retrieves his torch and makes his way to the fire pit. I stand back as he leans into our makeshift fire and ignites the planks. Our paper bags shrivel to ash in seconds and float around, blowing gently in the tunnel's cool ventilation. Within minutes, a small fire glows, illuminating the tunnel and replacing the cool air with warmth and light.

I ease back to the wall and sit down, noticing my torch is already out. *Good thing we got the fire going.*

Sky slides down to sit beside me. "Have you heard any news about the Dwellers that stayed behind?"

My eyes flash to his. In the soft glow of the fire, his eyes are desperate, searching mine for answers. I know he wants news of his mother and Cia. If only I could tell him something hopeful, but I can't.

"I don't know," I whisper.

He runs his hands through his hair. "I need to find out if they're okay. If they're safe."

I want to reassure him they've probably hidden themselves even deeper inside the intricate tunnels, but I don't know, and a part of me feels confident that the EHC has done their best to kill or capture every last one of the Dwellers who had anything to do with the rebellion. I can't say anything.

"It should never have happened!" Emma yells from across the tunnel and marches away from Elias. Her shadowy fist pounds the side of the wall as she turns and sinks to the ground. Even in the dim light, her eyes glisten with tears.

Elias eases away to the wall, holding his head in his hands.

"I should check on him," I say.

Sky stands as I do but stays behind as I walk around the fire to Elias.

"Are you okay?" I ask him.

His brow is furrowed, and his jaw is tight. "My mother—the EHC will come for her."

I crouch at his side.

"I know she's prepared," he says. "Ever since Mason started forming a resistance, she knew there would be risks. She will do whatever she has to—"

I place my hand on his arm. He glances to where it rests and looks back up at me.

"I'm scared for her."

Beside the fire, Elias' dark eyes shine, and his tough exterior softens. I draw in a slow breath. "If your mother is anything like Mason or you, she'll be just fine."

Elias's lips force themselves a strained smile. "She does have a safe house. Maybe she went there."

"I'm sure she did." I glance back across the tunnel to Sky, who gives me a confused look.

As I stand, Talen comes closer to us. "I'm sure my family is secured by the EHC already. It's what they do."

A part of me knows Talen is right. Anyone connected to us is doomed. We brought so much suffering to the people we care about.

I twist away from Sky and Talen. *What are we doing here? Why'd we ever start this fight?*

"None of this is right!" Drape shouts. "We're back underground—this is where we *started*! They killed our friends, our family, our resistance. What are we doing here?"

"What choice do we have?" I yell back. "We'll get captured if we go back to the surface."

"Or killed," Emma moans.

"What, now you're giving up, too?" Drape asks, marching toward me.

Pulling my shoulders back, I step closer to him. His green eyes are full of fury now. He stands firm and juts out his chin.

"I'm not giving up," I say. "I just don't want to get killed."

"We can't keep running," Drape argues.

I shake my head. The thought of going back to that cell again makes me shudder.

"He's right," Sky agrees. "We're hiding like frightened mice in the dark."

I turn to face him. "I'm just trying to stay alive."

"None of us will be alive if we do nothing," Drape says defiantly. He turns to face the others. "We've made it to the capital city of the EHC. I never thought we'd get this far, and we have."

I flit my eyes from face to face. A part of me begins to wonder if Drape is losing it, or if he's the voice of reason. "You saw what they're capable of. Reinhart was right. His technology is superior to ours."

"That doesn't mean we *give up!*" Drape shouts.

"What do you want to do?" Talen asks.

"Let's take them head-on," he says.

My spine stiffens. I shake my head and look to Sky. This can't be a good idea.

"It's just a matter of time," Sky says. "Soon all of our friends and family will be found in the Slack, and the underground habitats will only be stripped of even more humanity as they lock it down. We have to fight."

I turn to Elias, waiting for him to say something, to take a stand against this suicide mission, but he's on his feet. His soft expression is gone, replaced by something more determined.

"The city thinks we're terrorists," I plead with him

"Then let's beat them at their own game," Elias whispers.

A slow smile spreads across Drape's face. "It's time to turn the tables," he says. "We have to make Ethos see the EHC for who they really are."

"How?" Emma asks.

I pull back my shoulders and center myself. My suddenly cleared mind winds through the options, but there's really only one sure way, and it's going to require every ounce of strength we have left to do it.

"We take out the EHC leadership."

Talen raises a brow. "How do we do that?"

"We take the fight to the Ethos headquarters," I say. "This time, we'll put *them* on trial."

CHAPTER 7

"IF WE"RE GOING to do this, we need to rest up." Emma's eyes flash to me. Hope shines there, and I know she's ready for payback. "I don't think any of us slept last night."

"Not a wink," Elias agrees. "But let's make sure we're not ambushed while we rest." He waves Talen and Drape to follow, and the three of them head back toward where we entered, picking up a few planks and other materials as they go.

"And try to put together some kind of meal," Emma says, reaching for Elias' bag for the food her cousin provided us with.

Emma steps closer to the fire, holding a sleeve of crackers and two apples. She continues to dig around in the bag and then hands me the orange I took from Karim's fruit bowl.

She begins to make a pile of what little food we have.

"Not much of a meal, huh?" I say to her.

"Why don't you prepare the sleeping area?" Emma suggests.

I back away from her and the fire, knowing she needs her space. Emma's a tough woman, but even she needs some time to grieve the loss of her cousin and process every horrible thing we've brought on her.

Sky gestures with his head toward the far corner of the tunnel. I follow him. The light from the fire isn't as strong here, but it's enough to see several beams leaning up against what looks like drop cloths.

"We can use these," I say, bundling the fabric up. I find three long pieces and a few smaller ones. "Back to scavenging, huh?"

"Old habits die hard." He takes one of the cloths from me.

"We made use of everything underground." I laugh. "It seems so sad now, doesn't it?"

"Not at all," Sky says. "How else would we have prepared for one day surviving in yet another underground tunnel, hiding from the EHC, all the while preparing to raid their headquarters?"

I shake my head. "I would never have thought we'd get this far. Did you?" I turn to look at Sky. His skin is flushed, and after a moment he reaches out to smooth my hair.

"I thought I lost you."

My stomach flutters and all the old feelings for Sky rush back. My chest tightens as I remember how the ops took him, how I thought he was dead, and the agonizing time that passed when I couldn't get answers.

He drops the cloth and pulls me closer. I press my hand to his chest and my pulse quickens.

"I don't know how this happened," he says. "We haven't known each other for long, but I can't imagine my life without you."

I wrinkle my brow. A part of me wants to hear these words from him, but another part is afraid.

"What's wrong?" he asks.

Lowering my gaze, I sigh. "I brought so much danger and pain to you. Before we met, you had a life. Your sister and you were safe, alone in the Slack."

"If it wasn't for you, I would never have found my mother. And alone isn't always as great as is sounds." He reaches down and tilts my head up, pulling me close.

His body is warm as he wraps his arms around me and leans in. His lips brush mine, and in that moment my worries vanish. I melt into him and press my lips against his, feeling the energy pass between us. Time seems to disappear. Only the crackling sound of the fire remains. In that moment, it's as if we both understand how close we came to losing each other.

Far too soon, Sky pulls back, and my mind suddenly shifts. I take a deep breath and look at him. "Love in a world like this is probably impossible."

He reaches for my hand, entwining his fingers with mine. "But if love is possible, there's no stopping it."

I try to let his hope sink in, but before I can even process what he said, the sound of boots thumping over the ground and voices brings me back to reality.

I step away and spin around to catch Elias' eyes from across the tunnel. He stops in his tracks. His shoulders drop and his gaze lowers.

I'm distracted as someone walks toward us. "I'll take first watch," Talen says.

I bundle up the cloth and head back over to Emma, handing one to her and another to Drape. Then I take the orange and small stack of crackers she offers me and hunker down beside the fire. Elias turns a dark glare toward Sky. Before either one can move to my side for the night, Drape sits beside me.

"How would you like your orange prepared this evening, Madam?" He grabs my orange and brings it close to the fire. "Medium?" He inches it closer. "Or medium well?"

Smiling, I swat him, grab back the orange, and peel it open.

"We should all get some sleep," Emma says. "We'll plan our next move in a few hours, when we have more energy and clearer minds."

I bite into an orange segment, savoring its tart-sweet juice and nibble on a few crackers. I force myself to take my time and enjoy what might be the last of the food for a while. Now that we're on our own, there's no telling how we'll survive. I'll need my strength to get through whatever comes next.

Finishing the meager meal, I rest my head back on the bundled cloth, mind racing between Sky's kiss and Elias' stormy eyes. I take a deep breath and try to relax. There's no point in worrying about it. Love will never work out—not in this world anyway. Instead, my sleepy thoughts drift to tomorrow. Images of ops, hovercrafts, and glass prisons flood my every thought.

I shake them off then turn my gaze toward the fire, listening to the soft, sleeping breaths of those around me. As I slowly close my eyes, I feel myself nodding off, dreaming of a world where there's no EHC.

CHAPTER 8

GUNFIRE BLASTS ALL around me. I spin as a bullet whizzes past my ear and three EHC fighters race past. Their images are a blur in all the commotion, but I follow them toward what looks like Mason's Resistance Camp.

I gasp and shake my head. In front of us, the buildings are on fire. The smell of soot and toxic black fumes fills the air. A boiling sun overhead pulses down on us. I wrap my hands tighter around the gun I carry.

"Let's go!" a familiar voice calls out from nearby.

I turn. It can't be. Beside me, Jase blasts off another round.

"Move forward!" he shouts.

Raising my shaky hands, I aim toward the ops in the distance who are beginning to fire back. My heart pounds as I fire off several rounds, taking out two, *then* three of them before they can advance.

"Go!" a woman's voice shouts. From behind a cloud of smoke Knuckles emerges, waving us to advance. Sweat beads on her forehead. Her tattered shirt shows the signs of wear from fighting. A gentle breeze blows her hair back from her face, almost as if in slow motion.

I take another step toward her.

"Fight," she orders and holds up her gun.

My jaw tightens. "I-I can't," I say. "We're all going to get killed. I'm going to get you killed. I can't do this!"

Knuckles narrows her eyes at me. "Suck it up. You don't have a choice."

I try to swallow and get a hold of myself, but the air is dry. The dusty taste of sand coats my tongue, making the moisture stick in my throat.

Behind me, someone says, "Before it's too late, Fin."

I spin around. Oliver stands eye-to-eye with me.

Before I can say anything else, Jase, Knuckles, and Oliver turn toward the camp. They take off, running full speed at the fight and blasting their guns.

A dozen ops rush through the camp gates. Knuckles takes aim and somehow blows half of them away. Bullets ricochet off the rocks behind me, pinging into oblivion. I shield myself from the potential fire and call out for my friends to take cover, but there's no stopping them. Jase fires and the rest of the ops fall like dominos.

"We've got this!" Oliver yells.

My shoulders drop with relief. They've survived. We've done it.

From a nearby transporter, four more resistance fighters emerge, rushing down the vehicle's stairs and heading straight toward me. I shield my eyes from the glaring sun, trying to see who's there when suddenly their forms take shape.

"Elias!" I call out, gasping for breath. "They've done it. They've taken the camp!"

Emma, Sky, and Drape rush forward. Each of them carries a gun. They're focused on something behind me when Sky yells out, "Take cover!"

My spine stiffens as I slowly turn to see Lacy standing at the entrance of the camp. She proudly wears an Aura uniform. A devious grin consumes her face.

"No!" I scream just as my best friend raises her hands.

In a flash, everyone else I care about falls to their knees. Their screams echo across the dusty land. Up ahead, Jase's hands go to his throat. Sky's eyes bulge. Drape writhes on the ground, clawing at his throat. Emma is on her knees, coughing up blood.

"Stop!" I shout, racing ahead, but my modified speed is gone and it's like I'm running in place. I can't get to them fast enough.

I finally pass Jase and Oliver, whose eyes are rolled back in their heads.

It's too late. I've gotten them all killed.

Up ahead lies Knuckles. I make my way to her side. She reaches out to me. "Keep going," she says in a scratchy voice.

I shake my head. "There's nothing I can do."

"If you don't finish this fight," she whispers, "nothing will ever change."

I stomp the ground and yell, then spin to take aim at Lacy's head. Just as I pull the trigger, my gun is ripped from my hands and flung to the ground. Lacy stands, looking much taller than I remember, and lets out a laugh. Every ounce of me wants to rip her to shreds, but as if they were frozen, my feet are planted firmly in the ground.

"How could you do this?" I scream.

She slowly works her way from the entrance to me. Each step is like she's more machine now than human. When she finally gets to me, her lips quirk into a wry smile.

"It's your fault, you know," she says.

"No." I try to catch my breath and cover my ears, but my arms are cemented to my side. I won't believe her. My chest heaves as I take in all the destruction around me.

"It is," she says. "None of this would have happened if you'd just given up. So much for Noble intelligence."

"You know that wasn't a choice," I say between clenched teeth. "You were once one of us. You believed in our fight."

"You don't get it, do you?" She presses her lips together and backs up. "You've hurt so many people, and for what? Not a damn thing."

Somehow my arms release and I stretch out my hand, touching her shoulder. "Please let me help you."

Lacy staggers back, sudden confliction etched on her face. "I—I can't do this alone," she stutters. "Please help me, Fin."

A warm flutter of hope fills my core and I step toward her, but as soon as I do Lacy's body convulses. She drops to one knee and her eyes roll back.

"Lacy?" I want to go to her, but my legs won't move.

Lacy's skin vibrates, and small tears open, blood seeping out. Countless cuts appear all over her body and a swarm of tiny metallic insects pour out into the air. Lacy falls to the ground like a wood plank, the cuts merging together until she's unrecognizable.

"Lacy, no!" I shout, swatting at the buzzing swarm that surrounds me now.

I manage to sift through the silver cloud of nanos and find Lacy's body disintegrating before me. Dropping to my knees, I desperately try to pull her body to mine. The swarm grows and just as I take a deep breath, they stream inside my mouth. I cough and clutch at my throat. I can't breathe. A fire rages through my chest.

"No!" I barely choke out as my vision fades.

***

I gasp for breath and shoot up, swatting around me. Something metal clatters to the ground next to me.

The bugs are gone. I flick my head to the other side, scanning the dark, quiet space. I'm not outside. Beside me is a piece of ripped apart metal. I look down at my bloodied hands.

"Fin!" Elias calls, rushing over to me. He gently takes me by the shoulders. "Are you all right?"

My head is foggy and sweat coats my skin. Is this real?

Elias is alive, but Jase, Knuckles, and Oliver are still dead.

I smack the ruined container away from me and turn to the tunnel walls. Burning embers blaze before me in the center of the corridor. This is what's real. I take a deep breath and try to center myself.

"You just had a bad dream," Elias says gently, pushing my hair back from my face.

I wrap my arms around his neck and stay there for a second, taking slow breaths.

"What happened?"

"We were back at Mason's camp," I say, pulling back. "Everyone was dead."

"Everything is fine. We're fine."

I nod, letting reality take hold. "They died because of me," I whisper.

"Who?" Elias asks, his eyes searching mine.

"Jase, Knuckles, Oliver. And what happened to Lacy— she should never have become an Aura op. I could have stopped her."

"You didn't make the decision for her. Lacy *chose* to go in that direction."

A part of me wants to believe that, but I knew what she was capable of. I should have taken care of it sooner.

Elias inches closer and carefully takes my hands. "You can't beat yourself up for what happened. This is war. We're going to have losses. People are going to get hurt. Some of us won't make it out alive."

I swallow and nod, trying to let go of the guilt. I lift my eyes to his. A part of me wants more from him. I lean in closer, but before anything can happen between us, I pull back and stand up.

"Where are you going?" he asks.

"I–I need to wash the blood off my hand. And I'm going to find Sky."

Elias slowly stands. "He's on watch. Been there for the last few hours."

"He probably needs a break then."

As I turn to leave, Elias reaches for me again. "I'm here for you," he says. "No matter what."

My head aches. I slip my hand from his and snatch my water bottle from the ground. I pour some water over my hand and realize the damage isn't that bad. Only a small cut on my palm. It's already healing over due to my modification. I rush past Emma and Drape, who are still fast asleep. Closer to the entrance, Talen sits against the side of the tunnel wall. His eyes are closed, and his head is tilted to the side. He draws in slow breaths. I try not to make too much noise as I sneak past him and continue to walk until I spot Sky at the end of the long, dark tunnel. The lights flicker and the cool dampness of the underground sinks into me.

He turns and smiles as I come closer.

"Can't sleep," I say, leaning against the wall. "Do you want to take a break?"

"Sure. Thanks." His brow furrows as he looks me over. "You okay?"

I shrug. "Bad dream. I'll be fine."

"Want to talk about it?"

Talking about it would only make me relive it. "Not really."

Sky reaches out a hand and strokes my arm. "Everything will be better once we get out of here. Being back underground isn't good for any of us."

I sigh. He's right. I never thought I'd have to hide in the darkness again. Every step we make forward feels like it's immediately followed by two steps back. "You'd better get some rest."

"You sure you're okay?"

I nod, and Sky turns and heads back toward our group. Finding a flat surface, I set my water bottle to the side and hunker down beside planks of wood and other makeshift items Elias managed to collect and had used to build up this barrier. Down the tunnel, the lights continue to flicker, and the stale earthen smell of the underground fills my nose. A shiver works its way up my spine as I wrap my arms tightly around my waist, wishing I was back with the others beside the comforting fire.

After a while the nightmare fades and my eyes begin to feel heavy again. I turn away for a second to stretch my arms and legs. I have to stay awake. I take a drink from my bottle and pour a little water into my palm, splashing it on my face. *Only a tiny bit longer and the others will be up. We'll be out of here and back to the surface.*

As I'm on my third stretch, the hairs on the back of my neck suddenly stand up. A strange feeling overwhelms me, like someone is standing behind me. My shoulders tighten, and all my senses perk up. I spin around, but not fast enough. Something heavy smacks into my head and I stagger back. Instinctively, my hand drifts up to the throbbing point of pain. I fight to stay conscious, but the room turns into waves and the pain brings me to my knees. As I collapse, the last thing I see are two blurry black boots.

CHAPTER 9

I REGAIN AWARENESS, fighting to open my eyes.

The tunnel is dark, but I can make out a blurry human shape. My stomach tenses as pain pulses in the back of my head. I reach up to feel the wet, sticky blood matted in my hair.

"Once a filthy mole, always a filthy mole."

My eyes widen at the familiar voice.

"Surprised to see me?" the raspy voice asks.

My shoulders drop. I twist from side to side and then try to crawl, but in a flash he's beside me, growling into my ear, his putrid breath warm against my cheek.

"Where do you think you're going?"

I glare directly into his beady, brown eyes. "How did you find us, Yasay?"

Yasay mutters as he drags me down a long, dark tunnel, farther away from the others. More than a few times, I slip in and out of consciousness. But I force myself semi-awake and kick and scratch at his hand. But with every attempt to free myself, he twists my arm more. Shooting pain sears through me until finally he stops and slams me against the wall. I fade out again.

I blink open my eyelids and he's leaning over me. My eyes widen. The pain in my head throbs. He taps my cheek with the back of his hand, a few times soft and then once harder. The stench of his breath makes me turn away and my stomach roils.

"The rat's awake," he hisses and straightens.

"Let me go!" I yank my hands and something metal clacks. Chains are wrapped around my wrists and locked around a pipe.

Yasay coughs into his fist, deep and guttural. The fit keeps going, and he takes several steps backward. "Shut up!" he finally yells back.

I try to twist my way out, but the chains are too thick.

Recovered from coughing, Yasay marches toward me, and I see he's wearing some sort of dark blue military uniform with body armor and tactical compartments holding who knows what. Grabbing my arm, he shakes it to make sure I can't escape, then retreats, hacking again. Sweat drips from his face and a clump of what's left of his black hair clings to his forehead. He smoothes it back over the top of his balding scalp.

"Not feeling so well?" I ask. That was probably stupid, but I kind of enjoy the dig.

He ignores me. His face turns red and he spits at my feet. "Disgusting Dweller," he mutters, then continues into another coughing fit. Same old Yasay. Same old miner's cough. Disgusting pig.

I try to shift my focus away from him and onto how to get out of here. Panic pulses through me. *I can't go back to that tiny glass jail cell.* I scan my surroundings, but nothing looks the same. I'm still underground, but in a dingy, crumbling tunnel. I glance over and spot a set of tracks along the floor—a transportation shaft, like where Sky and Cia used to live in the Slack.

Yasay turns back around, holding one hand to his chest. A smug smile spreads across his stubbly face.

I narrow my eyes at him. "Get me out of these chains."

He waggles a finger at me as if I'm a misbehaving child, then comes closer. I scuttle as far back to the wall as I can.

"Your little revolt has helped my standing in the world."

"What are you talking about?"

"Your liberation attempt was not so successful, but mine..." he pauses, nodding with a smug grin. "My place with the EHC has grown *much* bigger."

I lift my chin. "Then I guess you owe me."

Yasay laughs, revealing a row of yellowed teeth. He almost slips into another coughing fit but stops himself. "No, I can't return the favor."

He crouches down beside the wall, grabs a bottle of water from his own stash, and takes a long drink. A part of me wants to kick the bottle from his hands, but I'm not close enough. Plus, it wouldn't help me escape. Knowing Yasay, he'd retaliate with a punch and knock me out again.

Once he's finished drinking, he wipes his mouth with the back of his hand and steps closer again. "After your little rebellion destroyed my mining operation, I didn't have many options left." He frowns and shakes his head. "You almost took everything from me. You even tried to use me to escape."

"I wish I'd destroyed everything—including you."

Yasay's brow furrows. "The EHC held me accountable for your revolt. They didn't go easy on me. Not fun. Not fun at all."

I press my lips closed as he backs away into the dim lighting. The shadows it casts over his face make him appear more sinister than he already is. "Then, I helped the EHC track down your little resistance group to Ms. Nejem's settlement, and that did the trick. I earned my place on the surface. It's not much, but it's better than living like a mole. Oh, and thanks for taking such good care of my mod kit. It worked like a charm."

I grit my teeth together. The day Yasay appeared at Emma's settlement was one of the worst days of my life—the day Sky was captured and much of Emma's camp was destroyed. Nothing would please me more than taking Yasay out right now, but even if I did manage to get these chains off me, I wouldn't be able to get to him fast enough.

A part of me wants to rip that stupid grin off his face, but before I can say anything I catch the movement of several dark figures creeping like wolves along the shadows in the corner of the tunnel. I squint to try to make them out.

"Now I'm a lead op for intel on underground combatants," Yasay brags, pulling back his shoulders. "Much better than my measly role in the mining camp." He slaps his chest. "Now the EHC come to *me*."

"Good for you," I say snidely. "So, you've captured me. Now what?"

Yasay snaps his fingers. A moment later, two men and a woman outfitted in the same soldier gear as him emerge from the shadows. The woman's hair is cropped short. The two men are dressed in the black ops uniforms and carry rifles. Off to the side of Yasay is a stockpile of weapons, ammunition, and other gear. Apparently they came well prepared to battle it out.

"This is my special unit," Yasay says, introducing the others. "Yasay's Special Underground Task Force."

"Task Force?" I scan the small mercenary group. The men stand with their shoulders back.

The woman has one hand on a plasma gun holstered across her chest in a sling. "The four of you were sent to bring us back?"

"Or whoever survives," the woman replies.

I take a slow breath and consider my lack of options. "Just take me," I tell Yasay. "You don't need the others."

"Naw... we get a bounty based on finding *all* the escaped prisoners," the shorter of the male ops says.

Yasay raises his arms over his head and gently stretches. "I'll bring you back to the surface," he says, "don't you worry. But not just yet. There's no rush, is there?"

I search his beady, brown eyes. "What's that mean?"

"You'll be found guilty just as easily today as you will be tomorrow, but I'm in the mood to hunt some rats."

My eyes flit from face to face.

"What about you?" Yasay asks the woman beside him. "Are you in the mood to hunt the vermin that scurry around in this sewer?"

The woman smiles and removes her gun from the holster. She nods, and the other two men beside her turn to each other, their eyes gleaming with excitement.

"No need for *all* of them to stand trial," she says, pulling back the trigger of her gun.

"Yeah," Yasay growls. He turns to look at me. "I'll save this rat for the privilege of an EHC trial."

My shoulders stiffen. I try to twist free from the chains, but the more I struggle, the more it makes Yasay's group laugh. "Don't do this!"

"Sit tight, A298," he says to me.

The reminder of my number sickens me. That's not who I am anymore.

"Come on." He points to one of the soldiers and the woman beside him. "Let's go kill the rest."

"What about me?" the lanky male op Yasay left out asks.

"You. Watch. Her." Yasay jabs a finger from him to me. "Don't let her escape."

A second later, Yasay and his two chosen mercenaries disappear down the dark tunnel. My heart pounds. *I have to get back to the group. I have to warn Sky. Elias is depending on me.*

The remaining op plops down across from me. For the first few minutes, his weasely face is lined with anger. He even slams the butt of his gun into the ground, but then, after a while, he turns a cool eye to me. A slow grin spreads across his face.

I swallow and feel myself stiffen even more, knowing this op is going to take out his disappointment on me.

I've got to get out of here.

As the op slowly stands, I scan every inch of my surroundings and quickly calculate the time from when I was passed out to when I woke up, trying to figure out how far Yasay dragged me. In the shadows is a darkened marking. I squint to see it, making out 'A16'. 'A11' was marked on the wall near our camp. It's got to be no more than a quarter of a mile back based on how markings worked underground. Five to ten minutes to break free before they're ambushed.

"No one said you couldn't stand trial a little roughed up," the op says.

I lean back and scream "Help!" at the top of my lungs.

"Stop it," the op demands, his sly grin replaced by annoyance. "Keep that mouth shut."

"Please, someone, help me!" I yell louder.

"If you don't shut up, I'll jam my gun down your throat," he warns.

Good. Do it.

Opening my mouth to scream again, he marches closer, within three feet. His gun extended, but before he can ram it into my face, I lift my legs off the ground and latch them around the op's neck.

"W-what the—" the guard snarls, his eyes going wide with fear.

I squeeze tighter.

His gun falls to the ground. His hands reach up to try and pry me off, but there's no chance. In a quick flick, I twist to the side. There's a muffled *snap*, and then the guard's head falls forward and back. I slowly release him. He collapses to the ground in a heap. Dead weight.

"Now for those keys," I whisper. I yank my foot out of my boot and work it toward the op's pocket. It takes a little wrangling, but finally I feel the cold key chain between my toes. I pull back my foot, the set of keys dangling from my toes, and in one swift movement raise them to my hand. Working the key into the lock takes less than a second, and soon the chains follow, clanging to the floor. I grab the guard's plasma rifle from the ground and charge down the dark corridor, hoping I'm not too late.

CHAPTER 10

YASAY CAN'T REACH THE CAMP. The people there are all I have left, and I *won't* let him take that from me.

I race down the tunnel after him. My heart pounds against my rib cage as I sprint harder than I ever have before. My breath catches in my throat. Sweat trickles down my brow and my lungs ache, but I push back thoughts of the camp being caught off guard.

This can't be happening.

As I pass tunnel marker A12, the sound of gunfire erupts, followed by yells echoing through the tunnel. My chest tightens as I skid to a stop. If only I could have warned them, screamed louder, fought back harder, did *something* to keep them from being ambushed. Shaking off the worst of my thoughts, I jog closer.

Steadying my breath, I reach tunnel marker A11 and peer around the corner. Ahead of me Yasay and his two ops are at the camp's still-blocked entrance—*I'm not too late, there's still time*—moving around the planks and other building materials we used to fortify the camp. Yasay kicks his way in. The male op keeps his rifle up, targeting the front while the female op quickly finds a way over the blockade.

Gunfire cracks through the air again, but I can't tell which direction it's coming from. I swivel my head around but it's no use, there's too much of an echo.

"Get the grenades!" Yasay yells to the male op.

I cock my rifle and charge ahead, firing. One of my bullets pierces the male op through the side of the head. He falls dead to the ground. The woman pops around the corner to fire her plasma rifle at me. It misses, but the heat rushes past me, igniting a scattered pile of rags in the corner. I hurry to the side wall and rub the singed hairs on my arm. The acrid scent of smoke is everywhere, but the light from the fire gives me a better view of where the other two are.

"I guess I underestimated you, rat!" Yasay calls out from behind the cover of fallen debris. My eye flits from where Yasay hides to the woman who's just as determined to drop me.

"You better give up! I won't back down!" I yell, pressing my back against the cool tunnel wall. Elias and the others have to be advancing. "You think you guys can hurry?" I mutter under my breath, unsure if I can handle killing both Yasay and the female op without their help.

A moment later, something shiny rolls up beside me, stopping right before my feet. I leap to the side just as a bright burst illuminates the tunnel, but the blast slams me into the ground and my chin rams into a rock, dirt filling my mouth. Grappling in the dark, I search for the rifle with shaking hands. Up ahead, I spot it, scramble to pick it up off the ground, and spin in the direction where I think Yasay and the woman are.

But they're not there.

Above me, part of the ceiling crumbles and a new, wide crack lines the wall. Beams that had only moments before been securely part of the tunnel now jut out at odd angles. I squeeze my eyes shut and try to refocus my mind on the exact location of Yasay and the female op, but as soon as I stand, the female op charges, roaring.

I raise my rifle and clock her right below the chin. The force of it knocks her to the ground, along with my weapon, which slips from my sweaty hands, but she bounces back to her feet as if she's got springs in them and sends a quick one-two punch at my face.

"You don't have to look pretty to stand trial," she says as I try to shield my head. "You just need to not die."

There's no escaping her blows. My mind spins, and to stay conscious I bite the inside of my cheek, feeling the blood trickle into my mouth. *I have to fight back.*

She raises her fist to strike me again and I brace for the hit—but it doesn't come.

I slowly raise my head.

The woman's eyes glaze over. A stream of blood trickles from her head down to her arm. A second later, she falls into a heap on the ground beside me. I gasp and struggle to my feet.

Behind her stands Elias, gun still held midair. "Are you okay?"

"I'll be fine," I say, spitting blood to the ground. "What took you so long?"

Elias steps closer and looks me over. "She got you pretty good."

"Nothing I can't handle." I still feel woozy, and the pain of the op's beating begins to surface as I press my hand to the wall to steady myself.

"Get your hands up," Sky orders, yanking the gun from Yasay's hands while Talen wraps wire around his wrists, then tugs Yasay to his feet.

"What do you want to do with him?" Talen asks, looking my way.

"We should kill him, but he could be of value to us," I say, wiping at the blood dripping from my chin.

Sky comes closer. "You're hurt."

"It's nothing."

"Come on," Elias says, his eyes burning as he glares at Yasay. "We need to regroup."

Before we can move, Emma and Drape emerge from the camp. A dark look rises over Drape's face the moment he sees Yasay.

"We can't get rid of this jerk," he growls. "He's like a cockroach."

"Save it," Yasay growls. "I don't care what you Slags say. Your little underground rebellion here is going to be found in no time. Just because you caught me doesn't mean *you* won't be caught, too. Once a rat, always a—"

"No!" I yell as Elias lands a good punch straight to Yasay's nose without warning.

Yasay crumples to his knees. "My nose!" he cries. "You'll pay for that."

Elias' brow furrows as he leans over him. "That was for my uncle Mason." He turns and walks away.

Yasay rolls over, wipes blood from his nose, and then slowly makes his way back to his feet. "I guess you're all one big happy family now, hiding like the rats you know you are."

"You have a lot of nerve," Emma says.

He shrugs. "We all do what we need to do to survive. I'm no different than the rest."

"You stand for nothing," I say. "You're only fighting to save yourself."

"That's because I'm important. Not like you common terrorists. The EHC believes I can catch dirty Slags like you. I won't let you take that away."

Is he stupid?

A part of me wonders if Yasay *wants* another punch in the face. I glance over to Elias. He tightens his jaw and clenches his fists again, then marches closer to Yasay.

"Wait!" I reach out for his arm and pull him to the side of the tunnel. Elias's eyes are dark storms. "We can use him," I whisper.

Talen yanks Yasay's head back and raises his hand at him. "You move, and I'll flood pain into every cell of your pathetic body," he warns.

I lower my voice and press myself closer to Elias. "I know we can't trust him, but we'll use him to gain access to where we need to go. Then we can get rid of him"

"I guess we don't have a lot of options," Elias mutters, glancing back to Yasay.

"You have *no* options!" Yasay shouts. Talen jerks his arm to keep him quiet.

Emma marches over to Yasay's gear and rifles through it. A moment later, she pulls out restraints and a communications device. "This is exactly what we need," she says. "We can hack into his device and intercept the EHC secure channels. It will tell us what we need to know to get us out of here." She tosses the restraints to Sky, then returns to digging through the gear.

Sky secures Yasay's wrists with the stronger metal bracelets and removes the temporary wire. "No escaping now, huh?"

Yasay's face relaxes. "If you want to get out of the city, or do *anything*, you'll need to take me with you. I can show you—"

Without warning, a loud *pop* sends me reeling back. I turn to see blood splattered onto the tunnel wall, flecks on Sky and Talen. Yasay falls back to the ground, his body leaning half-crumpled against the wall.

"What the—" Sky yells, backing up.

I rush toward Emma, who holds a gun pointed at Yasay's lifeless body. "He was going to take us out of here!"

"No," she says in a calm voice, lowering the weapon. "He wasn't. He was a waste of a life. He won't infect our plans anymore."

Talen backs away from the body while Emma takes the communication device and heads back to the camp. No one says anything as dread fills the area.

Elias's eyes are vacant, and he shakes his head. "We better take their gear with us," he mutters. "And look for food." He walks toward the woman he shot and grabs her plasma rifle. Talen pockets a few flash grenades while Drape collects their food bars and water.

"You okay?" I ask Sky.

"Great." He wipes the specks of blood from his face with his sleeve then plants his hand against the tunnel wall. "What about you?"

"I'm fine," I say, stripping the other op of his weapon.

"The upside to this," Drape says, coming closer, "is that we have more food and water now. We could probably last another few days down here."

"No way," I say. "We may not have Yasay to lead us out of here, but there's no way I'm going to spend another night in this tunnel."

Sky nods. "Agreed."

"There was no other option," Elias chimes in as we head back to the camp.

"What does that mean?" I ask.

He sighs. "Emma was right. Yasay would have found a way to sabotage us the minute he got the chance."

"We could have traded him," Drape says. "You know, as a hostage or something."

"Like Reinhart really wanted him," Sky says. "He'd probably have put a bullet in his head long before Emma did it if he didn't think Yasay might stand a chance of finding us."

I check my gun to make sure there are bullets in it, then head over to Emma, who's tinkering with the communications device. I watch in amazement as she pops open the back and fiddles with the wires. She gently pulls out two blue wires, cuts them, and then connects them deeper into the device.

"I'm in."

The others join us and listen as she secures the back and taps on the digital display to hone in on the EHC's chatter. Mostly what comes out are garbled voices and static, so Emma works on the display again.

"It's more difficult to get a clear transmission underground," she says, "but I think I can."

A few moments later, the static fades and the overlapping voices separate until there's only one man speaking.

"*The combatant's location has been found.*"

The hairs lift on the back of my neck and my eyes flash to Elias.

"*Commander Reinhart has been sent in.*"

"What?" Drape gasps. "We've got to get out of here. They're already on their way!"

Elias grabs the bag of salvaged gear and slings it over his shoulder. "We have to move. Now!"

My thoughts come rapidly as I follow the others. *Run! Don't stop! They're on their way!*

We manage to get three tunnel markers away before an explosion rocks through the air ahead of us, sending tunnel fragments crashing to the ground. Ten feet in front of us the ceiling dangles in jagged pieces. The walls of the tunnel lay in crumbled piles. Smoke, dirt, and dust swirl toward us.

There's no escape.

CHAPTER 11

"WE HAVE TO keep moving!" I shout.

"How?" Drape wipes dirt from his eyes. "If we go back the way we came, we're dead."

I grit my teeth and clench my fists. *We can't be caught again.*

"We don't have a choice." Elias steps away from the fallen debris. "We have to go back."

My stomach clenches at the thought of running for my life again. I slowly rise, keeping one hand pressed against the cold tunnel wall and the other on my chest in the hopes I can somehow slow my panic.

Just as we turn, another explosion rips through the ceiling and side walls of the tunnel. I fall back into Sky's arms. Elias, Drape, and Emma step closer together as a flash of fire shoots out of the wall.

"Relax," Talen says. He steps closer to survey the damage. Wires dangle and snap with electricity. "The tunnel is still stable enough."

Even so, there's the smell of something burning in the hollow space above the tunnel, and black smoke begins to gather in the updraft.

Drape coughs and holds his face to his sleeve. "What now?"

I settle my nerves and run my fingers through my hair, analyzing the possibilities of escaping this disaster. They're not good.

The comm in Emma's hand crackles to life. *"Heat signals have been detected,"* comes an op's monotone voice. *"The group has been detected near tunnel marker A15."*

"We need to find water—now," Emma urges.

Drape pulls at his shirt. "What? We need to get *out* of here!"

Emma scans the tunnel. "Not with the heat detectors. We won't get far with that tech. We have to find a way to cool down and trick the sensors. It's the only way to throw them off from finding us."

"But, there's no water down here," Drape protests.

"What about the sewage shafts?" Sky rushes to the end of the tunnel. Several cracks run lengthwise down to a grate that covers an opening at the bottom of the wall.

Sewage shaft? I cringe, but what other choice do we have? "Hurry," I say to him. "Open it up."

Sky rips off the grate. He sticks his head inside and then sits back on his heels. "It's old," he says.

"The water has been sitting there for a while. Maybe a few years."

"We'll take our chances," Emma says, holstering her gun.

"There's only a few feet of space." Sky slowly stands. "The chamber's clogged up, so we'll have to all squeeze in tight."

"It'll have to do," Elias says. "Just don't get it in your mouth if you can help it."

He moves Sky aside and climbs in. I hitch up my pants and sling my gun over my shoulder. One by one, we follow Elias into the dark, dank tunnel. The smell of stale, filthy water invades my nose. My stomach heaves, but the water feels strangely cool, and I know it'll only be a matter of minutes before all of our body temps drop.

"Close it," Emma orders Talen once he squeezes inside.

He pulls the grate closed behind us and suddenly we're immersed in a three-foot-wide chamber, closer to each other than I'd ever thought we'd be.

I try to focus on staying quiet while the sewage soaks into my pants and dampens my shirt and hair.

"Someone's coming," Talen whispers.

Between his arms, dim light shines through the grate's slats. I hold my breath and steady myself against the side of the chamber. The sound of clunking boots echoes into the tunnel just beyond the grate.

"Get someone down here to put out that fire!" a male voice yells. "Move those beams. Get through and *find* them!"

It's Reinhart.

A shiver runs up my spine. After a few moments, there are more sounds of boot soles hitting the ground—the ops darting from side-to-side just outside the grate.

"This has to end now," Reinhart calls. "Where are they?"

My chest tightens. I press myself harder into the slimy wall and shiver.

"Our heat sensors had them targeted to this point," an op from farther away shouts, "They must have backtracked deeper into the tunnel before the second explosion."

"I don't care if there's a trial anymore," Bellaton says through a comm. *"I just want them purged from Ethos."*

Reinhart growls and clicks the comm. "We can all agree on that."

"Then do it!" her voice growls, then cuts out.

"What are my orders?"

I close my eyes and wince. That's Lacy's voice.

Beside me, Sky's hand creeps into mine. I slowly turn my head. My eyes search his. He must know it's her, too. I bite down on my lip and turn back to face the grate, waiting for them to find us any second.

Reinhart slams something, maybe his fist, against the tunnel wall. The sound of it seems to vibrate deep into my wet skin. "I've had enough—kill them on sight."

I strain to get a very limited view of them through the slats. Lacy pulls back from Reinhart and opens her mouth to say something, but nothing comes out. A split second later she clamps her mouth shut and nods. "Yes, sir."

The pounding in my chest is almost too much. I'm sure Reinhart will hear it. A bead of nervous sweat trickles down my forehead and drips into the water. My eyes dart from the grate to Emma and Elias, wedged deeper into the chamber.

Reinhart directs several ops toward one of the tunnels up ahead, then orders the others to clear another path. A few moments later the noisy tunnel grows quiet. I squeeze my eyes shut and try to assess if it's safe enough to return to the tunnel. Before I can say anything though, Elias orders us back out.

"We don't have much time," he says, waving us forward.

Talen pries open the grate and we climb out. I've never been so grateful for clean air. I take a deep breath. Every part of me reeks of scummy water. Thick slime clings to my body, and I run my hand over my clothes to wipe off as much as I can. The others do the same while Elias replaces the grate.

I check my gun. "Did you hear Lacy?" I ask Drape.

Drape raises a brow. "Yeah. She hesitated."

"Somewhere inside her, she's still there."

Sky smiles. "See... same defiant girl you've always known."

I nod. "We have to get her back."

"If she's not reprogrammed," Talen says, sliding back into his boots. "There's no chance you will get your friend back. Don't even think about trying to reason with her. It won't work. She's blinded by the nanos."

"Talen's right," Emma says. "Confronting her now would be stupid. It could only get us all killed." She presses the receiver on the comm. A moment later, the chatter begins again, announcing their location.

"They're heading deeper into the old tunnel network," Elias says.

"Let's get out of here," I say. "It feels like we're in a giant trap. A maze of tunnels. If we stay down here, they're going to find us one way or another."

Drape shrugs. "At least outside we could hide better. Get out of the city or something—"

"We can't leave Ethos." I wipe a smudge of dirt from my arm.

"I'm tired of hiding all the time from the EHC," Drape adds. The non-stop fighting is wearing all of us down.

Emma taps the comm's display. "There's an EHC data center nearby. Maybe we can go there."

"Shouldn't be hard to get access to that," Talen says. "We could get in and regroup, figure a way out of here."

"Maybe we can hack into the system and get off their radar," I suggest.

"Good idea." Elias zips up the gear bag and follows Emma ahead.

There's nothing but tunnel for what seems like forever. Using the comm's navigation system, we walk at least twenty tunnel markers. Everything looks the same—lights, tracks, and lots of building materials as we move toward a staircase up ahead. Slinging my gun over my shoulder, I grab hold of the rails and begin to work my way up, following Sky and Drape as we quickly climb from the cold darkness of the underground into a lighter, more industrial part of the tunnel system beneath Ethos.

"Is that the data center?" Drape points to a door ahead where a bright light shines from behind a window. An access system is built into the wall beside it.

"How do we get in?" Sky asks.

Emma presses her lips together. "Maybe the comm will give us access." She begins to configure it again, tapping on the display and accessing its operating system while we catch our breath and look around. "A bit of reprogramming and I can make this device emit an EHC command token. That should get us in."

I gnaw on the inside of my cheek, glancing back down the staircase to make sure no ops have followed us.

"Got it," she says. Emma holds the device up to the access system. A moment later the door slides open and we rush inside.

We're no more than five feet in when a guard's voice calls out, "Stop there!"

My eyes flash to the guard, who quickly jumps to his feet from behind a desk. A second guard appears from behind a wall of flashing displays and panels. They're non-EHC guards, but still a threat.

"We've got this." Sky waves to Drape and they rush ahead with their guns drawn. The first guard holds up his hands. With one swift move, Sky knocks the guard out with the butt of his gun.

"What do you want?" the second guard demands.

Drape marches forward, backing the second guard into a corner, then slams his gun across the man's head, knocking him out in one blow.

Elias rushes to a half-opened closet and swings the door wide. "Get them in here."

Sky and Drape drag the guards inside. Drape locks the door and leans against it, breathing hard.

"You okay?" I ask.

"I'm getting tired of all this," he says. "I don't want to have to keep hurting people."

"None of us want to be doing this, but we have to keep going."

He sighs and turns his gaze to the massive room where we stand. "What is all this stuff?"

Emma heads to a giant display terminal in the center of the room. "It's amazing," she breathes. "A holographic data center."

"I can't believe it," Elias says.

Emma shakes her head. "Neither can I. In twenty-five years, the EHC has certainly made progress."

Tech devices surround us. Green light glows from crystal-like cubes, illuminating the machines around us. The room is cool and charged with energy.

My gaze moves from one instrument to the next. "How does it work?" I ask.

Running a hand along the side of a machine, Emma explains, "The data cubes are connected to quantum computers. The laser lights can access every possible dimension, providing massive data storage."

Elias steps closer to one of the beams of light. "They've managed to connect their entire force and every possible bit of information they can get their hands on."

Emma stares in amazement. "In all my years, I've never seen such a powerful system."

We move deeper into the facility. My mind scans the breadth of the room, what must be three thousand square feet of advanced systems. I open doors and examine everything.

"How long do you think we have?" Drape asks. "You know, before they find us again?"

"We shouldn't stay too long," Talen says. "The cameras will triangulate our location soon."

One of the doors opens to a bathroom. I head inside and use the sink to clean as much of the sewage from my hands and hair as I can. There's no sense in pretending it's all going to come out any time soon, so I quickly wrap my hair back into a tight bun, grab my gun, and head back out to the others. Just beyond a wall of storage systems, Emma stands tinkering with a digital device.

I make my way to her. "What are you doing?"

"Trying to hack the network terminal."

Ahead of us of us, information flashes on the screen—a series of numbers and code.

"What *is* all of that?"

"It's classified root data." She stops scrolling and points to something on the screen. "There."

"What?" Elias asks as he and Talen head over to us.

"There's a deeply buried directory with classified briefing reports. They didn't want anyone to see this. It's using old encryption protocols. Luckily for us, I was around when this encryption was commonplace."

She's brilliant, and not even modified. Amazing.

Emma leans in and reads, "'The EHC has been in a growing conflict with a large conglomerate from what was formally Asia.'"

"Formally Asia?" I echo, raising a brow.

"Countries fell into disarray during the Flip," Talen says, as if he's pulling up old records from memory. "The standard old-world politics and geography were re-written as new powers emerged from the ongoing chaos and destruction."

"Keep going," Elias tells Emma. "What else does it say?"

Using her hands, Emma slides screens and pulls up three more. "Here, 'A group called the Sovereign Nerics Alliance has long argued against the EHC's treatment of its people. For years, they have been peacefully engaging with the EHC to change their ways, but the EHC has denied them and banned all access to their region of the world.'"

My breath catches. *There are others who disagree with the EHC.* I turn to look for Sky. He and Drape head toward us. A smile broadens over my face. Maybe there *is* hope.

"There." Elias points out something to Emma. "Bring that up."

Emma widens the screen. "'Recently, the SNA has been moving on the EHC territories to offer aid to those left behind by the EHC,'" she reads.

"What?" Drape says. "Who's offering aid?"

I turn to face him. "Another organization— maybe one that's as big as the EHC." My eyes flash to Elias. "I never thought any one group could survive the EHC's attacks."

"We did," Elias says.

I turn to Emma. "Can we communicate with the SNA?"

She shakes her head. "It's impossible from this data center. They've blocked any chance at communication with them. I'm sure the EHC has regulated communication use to only its territories."

Drape eyes the comm in Emma's hand. "I think we should check it again, you know, just in case they're on their way or something."

Emma presses the display. Again, the familiar chatter begins. The ops' voices overlap each other. Each reporting back more information to Reinhart.

"They're getting closer," Talen says. "We have to move."

Elias picks up the gear bag.

"No." I cross my arms, refusing to budge as the others gather. "We need to act now. No more hiding."

Sky comes back to my side. "How can we? It's just us. You saw how many of them there are."

"We can do it. We've done it before. They're not going to stop. I'm tired of running, and I'm not going to do it again."

Emma raises a brow and smiles. "What do you suggest?"

"We still take on the EHC headquarters, but we're not putting them on 'trial' anymore," I say. "We need to destroy the leadership, starting with Bellaton. Sever the head of the beast."

CHAPTER 12

"No holding back, huh?" Sky says to me, a wry grin spreading across his face.

"It makes sense," I say. "We've been fighting for too long. Pretty soon we're all going to be exhausted from running. It has to be now. We'll take out Bellaton. It's the only way to make them understand they need to take us seriously."

Elias rubs his forehead, then drops the gear bag again. "We need a tactical plan to breach the EHC main building."

"The EHC headquarters?" Drape asks. "You mean next to the prison?"

The thought of the glass prison cell raises the hairs on the back of my neck. "It's Bellaton's operations center. She'll be there. Go for the jugular and the whole system will collapse."

"It was heavily guarded when we were brought there," Emma says. "There'll be even more guards now."

"But there will be fewer guards on the roof," Talen ventures. "If we start on top of the building next door, we can get across and work our way down."

"Easier than working our way up," I say. "As long as there's some way to get across." My mind flashes back to when Reinhart landed his helicopter. "I think there's a divide between the two buildings, but nothing we can't manage."

"Good," Sky says. "Let's go."

Emma flicks the comm device back on and it crackles to life. Voices tumble over each other, shouting commands. "Sounds like they're getting closer."

I raise a brow, trying to figure out how she can decipher one voice from another.

"Keep it on." Elias picks up the bag again and slings it across his chest. "We can take one of the side routes out of here. It'll lead us back to the surface."

We each take a minute to check our weapons and then follow Elias across the warehouse floor to a side door. He opens it, revealing another long hallway with grey walls and embedded lights overhead. We follow the corridor, which smells of must from the cold and damp. Talen picks up the pace, quickly leading us up the long, winding hall. Every nerve in my body is on high alert.

Soon, the dampness of the hallways begins to fade. I grip my gun tight and follow in Talen's footsteps. Up ahead, I can see an exit. The chatter on the comm device sounds like the ops are still running circles down below in the tunnels until the words, *"Data Center!"* come across loud and clear. *"They've headed out the east tunnel."*

Emma shoves open a door to the darkened outside. City lights glow and transporters zip above, bringing back a familiar memory of what it was like to reach the surface the first time we escaped from underground. A smile lifts my lips. I pull back my shoulders and take a deep inhale of the natural surface air. As we hustle through the darkness, I realize we've been underground for an entire day. Descended into darkness and emerged into the same.

"Let's take the back alleys," Talen orders. "We have to avoid the standard EHC patrol route."

Our feet pound the pavement. Sweat drips down my back as I clutch my gun to my side, ready to take out the first op who gets in my way. As we turn the corner, we run into a small group of fancily dressed people standing outside a shop. A few eyes flash to us and we quickly pull back. Further down the street, more citizens mingle near a pulsating sign that shows each one of our faces followed by the words: *"Dangerous. Criminals. Report immediately."*

Sky darts to the alley five feet ahead. The rest of us follow him, leaning against the alley wall, pressing into the shadows. I lean over to try and catch my breath to soothe my burning lungs.

"They saw us," Drape says. "Someone will report us."

"We can't... worry about that now," Emma replies between breaths. She holds the comm to her ear. "They're... out of... the tunnels. They'll be... right behind us... in less than a minute."

"Then we have to keep going," Elias orders. "No more stops. When we get to the research building, head straight to the back."

Before there's time to recover, we're off again, running full speed through the back alleys. Emma tries to keep pace as Drape drags her along. We emerge onto the main street only long enough to find another path that will keep us hidden from the EHC patrols.

"Two more blocks," Talen calls back to us.

I can only imagine what the citizens of Ethos must be thinking as they witness a pack of rebels sprinting down the street, guns in hand. One woman presses her back to the side wall. A stiff-dressed man pulls out his phone and frantically taps on the display. If only they could understand that we're trying to change things for the better, but their frightened stares tell me that unless we succeed in taking out the EHC soon, we'll never be thought of as anything more than the criminals Reinhart wants us to be.

The familiar sight of the EHC headquarters looms ahead. Its dark glass glistens even at night. Around back is the research facility attached to the headquarters.

Elias swings the gear bag off and takes out the guard who stands at the gate outside the entrance with a fast one-two punch to the man's gut. The op doubles over and moans as Elias sends a final hit to his head, dropping him to the ground. Drape picks up the bag and in one quick, seamless move we're through the gate and standing at the back of the research building.

Four ops appear from the back door of the facility. One yells to the others, and they rush toward us with their plasma guns drawn. My breath hitches as I raise my weapon and point it directly at the first op, ready to take him out, but before I can fire a round he's down. The other three ops follow him, each writhing and screaming in pain. My eyes jump to Talen, who stands rooted to the ground, his arms raised, and eyes focused in concentration.

I freeze as flashes of what Talen did to us back at Mason's camp fill my head. When it's finally over and the ops are dead, I grit my teeth, brush away the thoughts, and follow him with the others in v-formation as we enter the building.

"We can't have more than ten minutes," Emma says. "They'll be more ops who will check on the ones Talen just took out."

Inside, the building is cool and quiet. I scan for a way to get to the roof.

"Stairs," I shout, leading the group toward the far corner and heading up several flights. My leg muscles tighten and a twinge of pain stabs at my side, but I keep climbing until a door bangs open on the landing ahead of me. An op fires off a round. I duck, feeling the bullet whiz past my ear, then return fire, taking him out with a clear shot to the chest.

"Nice," Sky says.

We travel up another two flights, the echo of several pairs of boots pounding down the stairs ahead of us. Elias and Sky rush up first. Emma presses her back to the wall as rattling gunfire echoes around us.

"All clear," Elias calls out.

"I...don't know if I...can keep up," Emma gasps, hunched over, fighting for air.

Drape puts her arm over his shoulder. "I've got you."

She nods and exhales fast, determination filling her eyes. I smooth back my hair and continue to climb. My heart beats hard against my chest. I'm desperate for a drink to quench the dryness in my throat.

"Are we almost there?" Drape asks, his face red and dripping with sweat.

Talen opens the door at the top of the long, winding staircase. *Twenty floors*, I count, looking down. *Another twenty to go.* "We have to find an elevator."

Emma tilts her head for us to follow Talen through the door.

"We're halfway," Elias says as a man in a white coat turns the corner. His eyes widen as he turns to run.

"Leave him!" Talen says, pointing to the row of elevators along the wall.

Just as one's doors are about to close, Sky shoves his arm through and stops them. They slide back open and we rush in.

As the elevator speeds up, I take a second to try to catch my breath. I grab the water bottle from my pouch and down what's left in it. The others do the same as the floors fly by faster and faster. Suddenly, the doors open at the top floor, letting us out on the roof.

Outside, the cool, night air hits me with much-needed relief. I take a deep breath as we move toward the edge. Above, the stars fight to penetrate the glow of the city, reminding me how good it feels to be a part of the surface world. I gaze at the city beneath us. The light pulses from windows as vehicles zip through the winding city streets, reflecting off the surrounding buildings. A soft yellow glow illuminates the sky, as if the whole city is electrified whether day or night. Further in the distance, large machines work on new buildings, spreading the ever-expanding Ethos.

This city sparkles like thousands of stars.

As if understanding my thoughts, Sky reaches his hand toward me. His fingertips brush mine. Before I can say anything to him, a piercing alarm cuts through the night air. My shoulders stiffen.

"It's the breach alarm," Emma gasps. "It's coming from this science building."

"We don't have time to wait," Elias says. "We have to jump."

"Jump?" Drape gazes at the huge space ahead of us.

Moving to Elias' side, I survey the distance. "It's our only chance to get in there, but it's going to be a hard landing."

"Over here," Talen calls out.

We move toward where the building's roof extends out. "This is the best jumping point."

Again, my mind calculates. "Twenty yards," I say. "It's still a risk."

Emma steps back. "I won't be able to make it," she says. "I'll stay back and keep them occupied."

"No way," I say to her. "We can find another way."

Drape pulls close to Emma's side. Still out of breath, he says, "I'll help her. You guys gotta go."

"It's not happening!" I shout over the ringing alarm. "We're *all* going to do this!"

"Let me do this for you, Fin. I want to."

My heart tugs at my chest. Looking at my friend, emotions flood me as tears brim to the surface.

"Please," I beg. "I *need* you."

Drape smiles at me. "I'll see you again. I promise."

"We have to go, *now*," Talen urges. "The whole operation will be over if we don't."

"Come on," Elias orders me.

I turn to Emma and Drape and hug them both. "Please," I say, my eyes searching theirs, "stay safe. Hide, do what you have to, but please don't let them take you."

"We won't," Emma says, a reassuring tone in her voice.

Turning back to face the divide, my gaze falls on Sky. He furrows his brow.

"You okay?" I ask.

His jaw tightens. "Sure."

"Don't be nervous," I say. "We've got this."

He sighs. "Who's first?"

Before we can decide, Talen takes five steps back, then runs full speed toward the end of the roof, launching himself off the edge. My breath hitches. I want to turn away, but the strength in his body amazes me. His arms and legs flail as he easily covers the twenty-foot chasm and lands, rolling to the ground on the other side. He quickly gets back to his feet and waves for us to follow.

Elias backs up. He may not be as strong as Talen, but there's a fearless look in his dark, determined eyes. He runs toward the edge and sails through the air, landing with both feet on the other side, making it look like he's done this a dozen times before. His head twists back. He yells at us to jump.

I turn to look at Sky, but before I can say anything reassuring to him, he's already leaping across. "Sky!" I cry as he falls just short of the edge of the building, catching himself with both hands on the ledge and fighting to pull himself up. Talen and Elias are there in a flash, reaching over and pulling him up. Sky wipes his brow, stands, and waves for me to hurry, the three of them making room for me.

I rush back a few feet. My mind goes wild with calculations. My pulse races. Sweat drips down my cheeks. I swing my gun's strap to my back.

I've got this. Run, jump, land, tumble, go!

Sprinting toward the edge, I push off with every ounce of power I have in me. I feel my body catapult up as if in slow motion, and then I begin to fall in a perfect crescent, landing hard on the other building's roof, tumbling six feet to my side.

"Are you okay?" Elias asks, rushing to me.

"I'm fine," I grit out, standing and dusting off my pants. My hands and legs are scraped, blood dripping from torn skin. Nothing that won't heal soon. I push a stray hair from my face and glance back at Drape and Emma just as the door on the roof of their building opens.

"Run!" I yell to them.

The EHC ops waste no time firing off a dozen rounds. Bullets *ping* off the side of the building as Emma and Drape rush around the corner, taking cover near a large vent as they work on returning fire.

"We can't wait," Talen says. "We must go. They know what to do."

Elias pulls me through another door and into the EHC headquarters, toward what I know will be the hardest thing we'll ever do.

CHAPTER 13

AN ALARM BLARES, causing my shoulders to stiffen. Beads of sweat drip down my cheeks, and I try to stay focused as we race down a flight of stairs, but any second, we'll be swarmed.

"We have to get to Bellaton before she escapes," Talen says, rushing ahead.

"Wait!" I stop on the top stair, eyeing the next flight down. "Give me your plasma gun."

Without question, Sky hands me his weapon. I turn back, climbing back up to the rooftop door. I quickly fire off several rounds along the edges, and the red-hot flare fuses the lock, sealing it tight. The heated smell of burning metal fills the air. No chance of an air lift out of here for Bellaton.

"Get going," Elias's voice echoes back up the stairwell.

Rushing back down, I pant out the words, "The door is sealed," and hand the gun back to Sky.

"Good," Talen says. "Now, let's figure out how to get into the command center."

Without hesitation, the four of us charge down three flights of stairs. Our boots pound the hard floor and skid around each corner. At each doorway, I tighten my grip on my gun and brace for an ambush.

"Two more flights," Elias says.

My mind scans each level for where we last saw Bellaton. It's not two flights down. "It's here," I call out, coming to a stop. I immediately recognize the perimeter of the conference room down the hall. Just beyond that has to be the command center and her office.

Taking a deep breath, Talen swings open the door on this floor. Immediately, bullets fly through the opening, pinging against the stairs and railing.

"Close it!" Sky yells.

Talen slams the door shut. The sound of bullets hitting the metal on the other side continues.

I press up against the wall, calculating how many ops lay in wait on the other side. "There's five."

Elias and Talen nod. I know they've calculated the same.

"I'll take the one on the far right," Elias says.

Talen's eyes narrow. "The ones on the left are mine."

"Far end," I say. "I'll get him."

"What about me?" Sky asks.

"Get behind us," Elias orders. "Ready?"

I take a deep breath and yell, "Go!"

Again, Talen flings open the door. I rush through, blasting at the op in front of me. His body spins and drops hard. Elias stands in the door frame and takes out two guards charging from the right office area. They slide forward as their bodies go limp. With a flick of his wrist, Talen takes out the ones along the left wall. They crumple like someone electrified them.

"Easy," I say, swinging the rifle over my shoulder.

"Watch out!" Sky yells from behind.

Before I can turn, another op appears from around the corner. Sky raises the plasma gun and fires off a round of electric red light that pierces through the guard and fries him on the spot, but he's not fast enough. Just before he drops, the guard fires off a round.

Talen grunts as he takes the bullet to his left shoulder. His face tightens as he presses against the wall, dropping his gun. His hand flies to clutch the injury.

"Help him," Elias says. "Stay with him."

I rush to his side. "Are you all right?"

He slowly nods, but his clenched jaw and tight brow show that he's in pain. The bullet went clean through his shoulder and wedged into the wall behind him.

Sky and Elias move toward the front of the hall, taking out two more ops who turn the corner. The buzz of activity charges my body with adrenaline. I quickly scan around the corner just to the side of Talen. Ten more guards wait in formation.

"Careful!" I warn Sky and Elias, returning my focus to Talen.

"I've got it!" Sky shouts.

Blood drips down Talen's side. "Pull back your hand," I say to him. When he does, more blood flows. His hand is coated in red. "You need a tourniquet until your nanites kick in." I pull my pack over my shoulder and dig through it to find some loose fabric. "Can you use your ability to take them out?" A part of me knows it's selfish to ask, but another part of me feels like we're going to get mowed down without his Aura powers.

Talen swallows.

"I'll try," he whispers. He raises his hand and tries to concentrate. Sweat beads across his brow. His face twists in agony. After a few seconds, he drops his good arm to his side. "It's no use," he says. "I don't know what's wrong, but I can't connect to the nanites."

I quickly wrap Talen's wound. I tie it tight, but it's not enough. The blood soaks through. It'll have to work for now.

I shove his gun back into his hand and pull my pack over my back. "Let's keep going, okay?"

There's pain in his eyes as he shifts his weight off the wall. "We won't be able to get through them."

"What then?" I ask, running a shaky hand through my hair.

Talen's eyes go to a side door. "We can take them from the back."

My mind quickly follows his thoughts, and I recall a series of corridors, the same way they led us before stowing us in the holding center. It's the long way around, but it'll work.

I wave to Sky and Elias and point to the door. Sky slowly steps back and mouths, *Let's move.* He opens the door and we slide through, working our way quickly around the back hallways of the building toward the Command Center floor.

"How much farther?" Talen asks, grimacing. I turn to see his face is twisted in agony. I fall back to his side, wondering if the bullet somehow impaired his enhancement.

"It's there," Elias says.

Up ahead are double doors. Just like the tech operations underground, the area is secured. Two ceiling cameras turn toward us, the whirling mechanism zooming in to get a closer look.

"What do we do?" I ask breathlessly.

"Wait," Elias says. "Someone will come out."

"The cameras," Sky says. "They won't come out with the cameras on us."

"Let's see," Talen says. "All we need is one person."

We press ourselves against the wall. My head is full of chaos. A part of me wants to run back underground. Another part wants to finish this. Nothing would bring me greater joy than taking out Bellaton right now.

There's a metallic *click* and one of the double doors opens. An op steps out. Surprised, he reaches for his gun, but Elias grabs the end of his weapon and swings him around into the wall, knocking him unconscious while Sky holds the door open. These ops are Century class, so we have the advantage, and are one step ahead of them.

"Hurry," Sky says.

Elias rifles through the op's vest pockets. "He's got flash grenades," he says, pocketing two and handing off two others to Sky.

"No time like the present." Sky quickly pulls the key on each grenade and tosses them inside the command center, easing the door closed. A second later, a loud rumble roars from behind the door. Light illuminates through the window. The hallway's walls shake. A slow grin spreads across my face as I realize we're one step closer to Bellaton.

Several voices yell out as the doors fly open. The smell of chemicals fills the air and the taste lingers on my tongue and lips. Dozens of non-security personnel rush through the double doors. Women and men in suits dart down the hall, holding their shirts up over their mouths and noses.

"You sure that was just a flash grenade?" Talen asks.

Sky shrugs. The corners of his lips turn up. I shake my head.

We wait for the last of the office workers to rush out. Then come the ops. One by one, Talen and Elias take them out, dropping the disoriented guards before they even know what hits them. By the time they're done fighting, the hallway is littered with unconscious bodies.

"Come on," I say to Sky. "Let's get in there."

Before the last of the smoke fades, Sky and I are through the doors. Elias and Talen follow as we rush down a hallway and around a corner. Up ahead stands an op, who raises his gun toward us.

"Get back!" he yells.

My eyes flash to the door beside him. My mind processes what's behind it—*Bellaton's office.* I raise my gun. We fire at the same time. His bullet pierces the wall behind me while mine hits him square in the chest. He jerks back and slides down the wall, leaving a bloody trail.

The four of us stand outside the secured entrance to her office, each of our breaths only slightly muffled by the still-blaring alarm that sounds every few seconds and flashes red light around us.

"Use his hand," Elias orders.

Sky and Talen raise the guard's body to the access panel. I grab his limp hand and press it to the panel. When the door doesn't open, I try once more with his other hand. Again, nothing.

"It won't work," Sky says, dropping the guard.

"You need to go back," Elias says. "Secure the way we came. More ops will be on their way."

My eyes glance to Talen's wound. It's finally stopped bleeding and should be healed soon. Talen and Sky take off down the hall.

"What now?" I ask Elias.

He gazes at the door. "Maybe we can blast it open."

I raise my gun when a crackle from the door interrupts my thoughts. "What's that?"

Elias turns to the access panel. "Someone's trying to say something."

"I'm tiring of your little group," comes Bellaton's voice. *"This is a level ten rated security room. There's no way you can get to me."*

Anger pulses through my veins. I clench my fists and chew on my lip. No way I'm leaving without getting in there. Not after everything we've been through.

"You're nothing but terrorists!" she screams through the comm. Her voice is shrill and panicked, far from the lifeless, ultra-poised lady we originally met. It brings a smile to my face. We've got Bellaton cornered. She's afraid.

"You're nothing but a virus that needs to be eradicated," she snarls.

I find and press the comm button on the panel. "Why are you restricting access to the SNA?"

There's a pause. *"You know nothing,"* she hisses. *"You're in way over your heads!"*

Elias presses the button. "We're going to crack open the EHC territory."

I twist back and forth, wondering how much longer we can stand outside her office door before reinforcements power through.

"We've got to do something," I say, holding up the gun.

A moment later, Bellaton's voice returns. *"I'll allow you to leave unharmed. We will stop hunting you."*

My eyes flash to Elias. Empty promises that we've heard too many times before.

"No thanks," Elias replies into the device.

Stepping back and pressing my back into the opposing wall, I stare at the door ahead of me, ready to kick it down, but before I get the chance, Emma's voice crackles to life through the comm device in Elias' pocket.

"Elias?" Emma calls out.

His eyes go wide, and he pulls out the radio. He quickly presses the button. "We're here. Outside Bellaton's door."

"You've made it!" she says.

"Yes, but we can't get in. The room is secured."

"Give me a second. The EHC likes to track everything. Their communications network is integrated for optimal response times."

I swallow and grip my gun tighter. They underestimated us—like always. The sound of voices and muffled gunfire nearby raises the hairs on the back of my neck. "Hurry," I whisper, bouncing from foot to foot.

Suddenly, the door *clicks* open.

"You're a genius!" Elias shouts into the device.

"You're welcome," she says. *"If you run into any more trouble—"*

The rattling of gunfire takes over her words, and Emma's voice fades to nothing but static.

A huge weight presses against my chest. I rub a sweaty palm against my pant leg. "We should've never left them."

Elias looks back at me, his dark eyes full of concern. "She'll know what to do."

I nod, hoping he's right.

Holding up our guns, Elias pushes the door wide open. Smiling, I say, "Caught like a rat," and point my gun at a nervous Bellaton.

She stands behind her desk, her shaky hands raised, eyes shifting back and forth as she whispers, "Don't shoot."

CHAPTER 14

"Y-you can't shoot me," Bellaton insists. "They'll never let you escape if you do."

I step forward. "We'll take our chances."

Bellaton's eyes widen. She stumbles back into the wall. "Wait! Your friends are in our custody. That boy and Ms. Nejem. They're with Reinhart. If you kill me, forget about saving them. They won't stand a chance."

My finger traces the trigger. Nothing would bring me more joy than taking her out right now, but we still need her.

"Hold on," Elias says, putting his hand on the end of my rifle and lowering it. "She could be telling the truth."

Bellaton snatches the comm device from her desk. "I'll prove it to you."

Elias raises his gun in line with her head. "Be careful what you say."

Her hand shakes as she flicks the device on and holds it up to us. "Commander, put the woman on," she orders. "I've been compromised."

"Ma'am. Are you alright?"

"Do it!" she growls.

I swallow as my chest tightens.

"Fin, if that's you, don't worry about us. Do what you need to do!" Emma shouts.

"That's enough…" Reinhart snarls in the background.

A shuffling sound crackles through the comm and Emma is quiet.

"Emma?" I call out.

Bellaton slowly lowers the radio next to a computer terminal that juts out of the metal desk next to her. "There's not much time," she says, lifting her hands again. "Without me, they stand no chance. They'll be executed within minutes."

She's right. My mind flashes back to Bellaton and Reinhart's conversation in the underground tunnels. There won't be any trial. Their masks are off. No more phony attempts to look like a fair judicial system.

Voices from the comm on the desk come through. *"Two more spotted in the command center,"* says an op, then there's the sound of gunfire. My breath catches. It's close, too close, as if they're battling Sky and Talen near the entrance.

"We have to hurry," I say to Elias.

"Bring them here," he orders Bellaton, pointing at the device. "Pick it up. Now!"

She lowers her arms and presses her palms into the edge of her desk, lowering her head while Elias steps closer. My gaze bounces back and forth between the two.

"What kind of reassurance do I have from you if I do?" she demands.

"None," Elias hisses, cocking his gun. "You're not really in a position to negotiate right now."

Shouts come from outside the door.

"They'll be in here in seconds," Bellaton insists. "The ops will take you out."

Elias steadies his hand. "But I'll take *you* out first."

The pounding in my chest intensifies. "It's your best chance of getting out of this alive," I say to Bellaton.

She shakes her head. "No, no, no."

The tip of Elias' gun is so close to her that one shot would leave very little of her head intact. My hands go clammy and a dull ache radiates up my arms. "What are you waiting for?"

Bellaton turns a harsh glare to me. "You will not destroy the hard work the Enhanced Human Coalition has done. The only reason anyone has survived this long is because of us."

"On the backs of others. Your system doesn't work."

"It's worked fine for Ethos."

"There's a bigger world out there with the SNA," I say.

She shakes her head. "You don't know what you're saying."

I grab the comm device and thrust it into her hand. "The EHC's reign is over in this region. Tell Reinhart to bring our friends here *now*."

"You think you get to decide when the EHC should stop?" Bellaton growls. "How dare you? We've improved the world."

"Slavery and absolute control is not improvement," Elias says. "We don't have time to argue with you. Your choice is simple: call Reinhart and tell him to bring Drape and Emma here now or die."

A sneer replaces the anger on her face. "You've been running for a long time. Aren't you tired of all this fighting?"

Elias pushes the barrel of his gun against her temple.

Her eyes widen as she tries to step back, unable to get anywhere. "You can have a better life," she says breathlessly. "Walk away from this alive. Start again somewhere else. You must be tired. Always on your guard. Sleep deprived. Hungry."

I swallow and think about her words. She's right. I feel all of those things deep inside my bones.

I take a long breath in and exhale, then adjust my grip on my gun. There's no way I could ever give up now. Not when we're this close.

"We're done hurting people," I say. "You're going to open the lines of communication. We're going to reconnect to the world and rebuild."

Bellaton blows out a sharp breath. "The SNA isn't as great as you believe."

The sound of gunfire blasts from behind the wall. Voices echo through the vents and from back down the hallway. A trickle of sweat beads its way down Elias' cheek and the gun rattles in his hands.

"You need to get on the comm," he orders. "Now." His tone is intense—deadly.

Bellaton swallows, thoughts racing behind her eyes. She lowers her hand down to her desk and presses the display. "Reinhart," she calls out, "we have no choice. I am not in a position to compromise."

"We'll be there in two minutes," he shouts back.

Elias raises a brow. "Tell him to bring Emma and Drape to us."

She stiffens and folds her arms across her chest. I can't believe she won't do it. My pulse beats hard in my neck and arms. Aiming my rifle two inches to the right of Bellaton's head, I fire off a round.

She shrieks and covers her ears as the bullet blasts a hole in the wall behind her. Fumbling for the device, Bellaton presses the receiver. "Bring the terrorists to my office," she says, then lowers her head.

Elias steps back, but I keep my gun pointed at her. Bellaton slowly raises her head and rubs her temples.

The sound of shouts come from outside. I turn toward the door just as Sky and Talen step through.

"There's no way we can keep them out," Sky pants. His eyes flash to Bellaton sitting in the chair and the hole in the wall. "At least we have her."

"Exactly," Elias says. "And they're going to bring us Drape and Emma."

Talen reloads his gun. "What happened?"

"They were captured," I say.

"We need to end this here," Elias adds.

"You'll never leave alive," Bellaton says again. Her strained face tells me her whole world is falling apart. Everything she worked for is about to be destroyed.

Sky moves toward her desk, standing at her side while Talen shifts to the corner, both ready for another fight, if it comes to that. I know it would be disastrous if any one of us opened fire. The space is too tight. Nowhere to hide. A bloodbath comes to mind with all of us ending up dead in one last stand. I push back the thoughts and refocus on Bellaton, wishing they'd hurry.

Suddenly, the sound of boots pounding down the hallway echoes closer. My grip tightens around my rifle and Elias, Talen, and Sky aim toward the door.

Reinhart shoves it open. His face is red and lined as he turns a stern eye to Bellaton, burrowing his disappointment and rage into her. Behind him stands Lacy and three ops.

"Where are they?" Elias yells. "Drape and Emma. If this is a set-up, she's dead."

Reinhart's nostrils flare. "Relax. We did what you asked."

"Just bring them here," Sky says.

Nodding toward one of his ops, there's a scuffle in the hallway, then Drape and Emma are dragged around the corner and shoved into the room. My breath catches as I see them. Their hands are cuffed. A red welt covers Drape's cheek. Black bruises line Emma's arms and neck, but, feisty as ever, Emma turns and spits at Reinhart's feet. Drape inches into the corner beside Talen, his head hanging low.

"What did you do to them?" I demand.

"They're our prisoners," Reinhart says, glaring at me. "We'll do with them what we like."

Rage pulses through my veins. "If you want to play it that way," I say to Reinhart. I take a step closer to Bellaton and hit her under the chin with my rifle. She cries out. Her hands fly to her face as she rocks back in her chair.

Reinhart clenches his fists. "You'll regret that."

"Not as much as you will if you touch any one of us ever again!" I yell. My eyes jump from him to Lacy as she enters the room. Her face is stiff, robotic. Whatever is left of her humanity is buried deep beneath a cold, hard stare. If only she could be my friend again. I ache for her to be like she once was.

Lacy narrows her gaze. She raises a hand toward me. Elias turns to face Bellaton again, raising his gun to her. "Don't even think about it," he warns her. "Use your ability on us, and I *will* pull the trigger."

"This was foolish," Reinhart huffs. "You're in way over your heads. This won't end well for any of you."

"Maybe not," I say. "But if we die, so do you, and at least it'll be to free the Dwellers and the EHC civilians from your control."

Reinhart's jaw tightens. My words must hit him like the bullets I want to shoot into his chest. I return my attention to Bellaton. "Open a secure channel to the SNA leadership."

"You can't be serious?" Reinhart scoffs. "That would be a mistake."

Ignoring him, I demand again. "Open. The. Channel. *Now*."

"Your plan will never work," Bellaton says, a bit more timid now. "You don't know what it takes to survive out there."

My chest rises and falls. If I could laugh out loud right now, I would. "All I know *how* to do is survive."

Bellaton's eyes flash to Reinhart. He runs a hand through his hair. "Don't do it," he says.

Slowly, Bellaton picks up the comm device and hands it to Emma. "You'll have to do it."

Emma takes the device, holds it up to her ear, and listens to the chatter. She quickly changes the channel and listens again. "What channel?" she demands.

Bellaton presses her lips together, not about to give up the information. There's not much patience left in me. I march to her side, ready to shoot her. Maybe not in her head like I really want, but her arm or leg.

Before I can pull the trigger, Elias shoves his gun into her cheek. "We can do this the easy way, or the hard way."

Her eyes fill with fear. "Give it back to me," she says.

Emma hands her the device. "Find it."

Bellaton presses her thumb to the digital display. She flicks through the channels, then stops. "Command access F39RT009-delta," she whispers. She hands it back and Emma holds it up for us to hear.

The connection is clear and quiet. No voices, nothing.

"Where's this coming from?" Talen asks.

Lowering her head, Bellaton says, "It's an SNA digital signal. It's not EHC."

"Say something," Drape says to Emma.

She sighs and hands the device to me. "You should do it?"

"Me?"

"You made this all happen," Emma says.

Reinhart makes a slight movement toward the device, but not before I take it from her hand.

"Once you do this, everything will change," he says, staying put now.

"Good," I say. I've waited my whole life for change. I take a deep breath and press the receiver. "Hello? Is anyone there?"

Silence greets my first attempt. I swallow. My eyes scan each face in the room. A part of me hopes that all of this wasn't for nothing.

"Try again," Sky urges.

I press the button again, but before I can say anything a voice says, *"Sovereign Nerics Alliance secure channel, delta one. Please identify yourself."*

CHAPTER 15

MY BREATH CATCHES. I quickly press the button. "Fin—"

"Stop," Reinhart orders, raising his gun to my head. "You speak one more word, and—"

Elias turns his gun on Reinhart. "Don't listen to him. Keep going."

Sky takes aim at Bellaton, and all around us, the ops raise weapons. The small office space is charged with nervous energy. My eyes jump from gun to gun, and from the pounding in my chest my heart feels like it might punch its way out. I swallow and release the button.

"Kill her," Bellaton orders.

Drape pushes back into the corner, but Emma inches closer to me. "You do, and every single person in this room will be dead. Is that what you want?"

After a moment that feels like an hour, Reinhart slowly lowers his arm. He furrows his brow and mutters something under his breath. "Stand down," he finally says out loud.

Emma steps in close to me. "Give them our location."

I depress the button. "Command access F39RT009-delta. Enhanced Human Coalition. Located in the capital city, Ethos."

Bellaton slams her fist against her leg. "You've just destroyed everything," she hisses, looking to Lacy.

Lacy's eyes burrow into me. Motionless and stiff, she's in pure robotic compliance with the orders. She begins to project her mind onto us until Talen puts a gun to her head. "Back down, or else."

I gulp and grip the comm device tighter. *Do what he says, Lacy, please.*

She takes a step back and averts her eyes to the ground.

"Hurry," Emma says. "We have to make contact before it's too late."

No way I'm going to stop now. I've waited too long for this. I take a deep breath and then click the button again.

"My name is Finley. I'm part of an underground Dweller resistance. There's been an uprising. We've taken over the EHC Command Center." I flash a smug smile to Bellaton.

"You've made a calculated mistake," she says, narrowing her eyes. "Those modifications have made you delusional."

Sky moves his gun closer to her. "I don't think you're in any position to be insulting us right now."

"That's enough," Reinhart orders.

"I agree," Elias says. "The message has been sent. It's over. Now, let's get them out of here."

Talen moves to Reinhart's side. "Give me your gun."

Reinhart grits his teeth and doesn't move, but with our weapons trained on Bellaton, the commander finally relents. His shoulders drop as he hands over his weapon. "This isn't over."

Sky jabs his gun into his side. "Move it!"

"What about them?" Drape asks, pointing to the ops before Reinhart is escorted out.

Slowly, the commander nods. "Hand over your weapons," he tells the guards.

Drape takes their guns, each of their faces tight with anger. Lacy stands barehanded. My nerves settle as I pull back my shoulders and raise my chin. I can't help but worry about her. The longer she's an Aura op, the greater hold the nanites take.

"Everyone out," Talen orders.

One by one, Reinhart, Lacy, and the ops are pushed from behind until they gather in the hallway.

"I'll secure them," Elias says. "Try to make contact again."

"Let's go," Talen says to Bellaton.

The director circles her desk, glaring at me the whole way around. "You'll regret this," she says as she follows the others out into the hallway.

"Keep her secure," I say to Talen. "She's our only bargaining chip."

He nods.

Drape and Sky follow, leaving Emma and me alone to figure out the next step. I blow out a quick breath, grateful for how that went and that none of us fired the first shot that would have definitely ended everything in a matter of seconds.

"What now?" Emma asks.

I rub the back of my neck and press the button to call the SNA again. No response. I click off and pace. "Where are they?"

"Try again," Emma says. "Maybe the communication was cut."

Pressing the button, I repeat the coordinates of Ethos and retell the story of our coup. Elias returns from the hall and closes the door. "Sky and Drape have them secured in the office next door. Talen's watching the corridor. I don't know how long we have. More ops are probably going to storm the command center soon. Any word back?"

I shake my head. "Nothing."

"Well, we have to establish an open line," he says, wiping sweat from his head and checking his gun. "Without them, we're sitting ducks."

Emma pulls back the window shade. Just beyond the window, I spot a line of black uniforms on the roof next door. I chew on my lip, knowing no matter which direction we run, there will be a fight, and with each passing minute more guards will join in.

"We have to do something," I say.

"Let me try." Elias takes the comm device. "This is Elias Hayes. I am one of the leaders of the resistance movement to overthrow the EHC. I'm with Emma Nejem and several others. We are trying to make contact with the SNA. We need your help. Is anyone there?"

He holds the device between the three of us and we wait, but there's nothing but silence. Cool air from the vent overhead kicks on and ruffles my hair. I step back and turn to face the wall. If all of this was for nothing, I don't know what I'll do. After all the fighting and sacrifice, we can't just give up.

The device crackles and I spin around. Emma's eyes go wide.

Elias presses the button again. "Is anyone there?"

Another second, and then a voice says, *"This is Ambassador Garrett Morris. We've received your transmission and understand you are located within the city of Ethos, an EHC held territory."*

"Yes," I say, rushing to the device. A wide grin spreads across my face as I tremble with excitement.

"I handle communications with outside sectors," Morris says. *"We've been trying to regain contact with the EHC for several years. I'm glad you found a way to get through to us. I will assist you from here."*

"Thank you," I say. "We thought we lost contact."

Morris clicks back on. *"The line is secure. We had to verify the connection. After all this time, we were... a bit surprised to hear from you."*

Elias laughs. "It's good to make contact with you, sir. It's been a long road." He lifts his gaze to me. His eyes shine. In one fluid movement, I throw my arms around him. His arms are tight around me as he lifts me into the air.

Emma steps back to Bellaton's chair and sits down, resting her head in her hands. "Let's not jump the gun."

"What?" I ask as Elias lowers me to the ground.

"We don't know if we can trust them yet."

I sigh. Not trusting is ingrained into every fiber of my being. It felt good for one moment to have hope, to imagine escaping this nightmare and beginning again in a new world.

"Why do you say that?" I ask Emma, raising an accusatory brow.

"We've only just discovered this group. There are no guarantees that they can even help us."

Again, the device crackles and my eyes flash to it. Emma's words bounce around my head, making me wonder if our easy out might be more challenging than I thought.

"I've been tasked with mending relations with other regions and organizations," Morris says. *"I'll do my best to assist you in any way needed."*

Elias takes the device. "We need your help to get us out of here."

"We're not in the best situation," I add. "We've stormed the EHC command center and have captured the Director of Operations, Flora Bellaton. She's our only leverage to escape."

"I don't know her," Morris says. *"However, I'm sure you are very anxious to get out of there. From our past experience with the EHC, they won't let you go easily. The citizens of Ethos and the Dwellers have suffered a great deal, I imagine, manipulated under the control of this powerful organization."*

Taking a deep breath, I close my eyes. Hearing another person say those words brings me some validation. My shoulders begin to relax. Even though we still have to find a way out, I feel comforted that soon a whole new life will begin for us.

"I think we can trust him," I say to Emma, who furrows her brow. "We don't have a lot of options."

Emma sits silently and eventually opens her mouth to speak. "Ambassador Morris, what do you advise? We need to get a secure path from the building and out of Ethos."

The speaker crackles with static. *"I suggest you grant the SNA access to the no-fly zones,"* Morris says.

Elias steps back. "Can we do that?" he asks Emma as soon as she clicks off.

"We'd have to hack into the system or force Bellaton to do it," she says.

Morris' voice breaks in. *"They've been on lockdown for over thirty years."*

Thirty years? I begin to chew on my lip. Opening up the no-fly zone sounds risky.

"I'm not sure we can do that," Elias says into the comm.

"I can offer you support to secure control of the EHC."

My breath hitches. "We'll never be able to do that on our own," I say. "This might be the way."

As I try to take back the device, Emma grabs it. *"Wait.* We have to think this through."

I sling my gun over my shoulder. "What's to think about? It's our only option."

She turns to Elias. "Had you heard of the SNA before today?"

"No, but that doesn't mean anything. The EHC kept a lot of information secret from us."

"Ambassador Morris, this is Emma Nejem. We're prepared to assist you. However, I've been a part of the EHC society since I was a child and have never heard of your organization before today."

A few seconds of silence and the comm comes back to life. *"As you know, the EHC works hard to maintain order. It is our belief, that we and other groups have been wiped from your society's records. Letting the people know that there is something more out there is not in their best interest."*

The device clicks out as Morris waits for our response.

"Do you believe him?" Elias asks Emma.

Emma shrugs. "I have no idea. He's not telling me anything new."

"Then make him tell you something new," Elias urges, then clicks the comm back on.

"When did the communication end?" Emma asks.

"Several years ago," Morris says. *"The EHC has developed defense systems that have locked the rest of the world from their territory and comm networks. The EHC needed to look like the sole proprietor of the world after the Flip."*

"Why?" Elias asks.

The same thought runs through my mind. What would the EHC have to gain from convincing the rest of the world that they were the sole owners?

"Power," Morris responds. *"It's always been about power with the EHC."*

Emma lowers the device to the desk, flicking it silent.

"There's one thing that bothers me," Elias says, grabbing the device. "Ambassador Morris, how has no one been able to make contact for this long?"

"The EHC restriction zone extends far beyond all their cities' limits," Morris says. *"No one could ever get close enough. We have tried. Every attempt was met with retaliation from EHC forces."*

Emma leans back in the chair. Elias quickly covers the device to give us a bit of privacy.

"If only they had gotten through," I say. "This could have ended a long time ago." We toiled underground all this time when help was trying to get to us.

"We have to make a decision," Elias says. "Do we accept their help or not?"

Emma nods at the device and Elias removes his hand, holding it out. "What guarantees can you give us?"

"Once we enter Ethos," Morris begins, *"we can secure your safety."*

"What about the citizens?" Elias asks. "They'll blame us for this."

Morris clicks back. *"We'll help the others to understand your uprising. I understand you're nervous. There's only one way for us to help you; you must open the no-fly zone."*

"It's the best offer we've got," I say.

Elias grabs the device and opens his mouth to respond.

"Hold on," Emma says. "Don't agree to it."

"Why?" Elias asks, returning a hand to cover the device.

I turn a sharp gaze to her. "It's our only way out."

"No," Emma says. "It's not. We still have another option." Emma takes a deep breath. "Get Lacy back in here."

Elias wipes the sweat from his brow. He grabs the comm device. "We'll get back to you soon."

After a moment, Morris replies, *"Don't wait too long. This may be your only opportunity."*

Each of us looks to the other, recognizing the stakes. Elias checks his gun. "You want to reprogram her?"

"Can we do that?" I ask.

Emma's eyes shift to mine before scanning the room. "Maybe. The nanites are customized for each person. Just because we were able to hack Talen's doesn't mean Lacy's will be the same."

With Talen, it was hard enough, but Lacy was infused with the latest Aura nanos. She could be far more complex to break.

Emma jumps up from the chair. "We'll need some supplies," she says as she pulls open Bellaton's desk drawers, then moves over to the cabinets.

"Like what?" I ask, scanning the room.

"These," she says, holding a couple of stun weapons.

"Where did you find those?" Elias asks.

"Here," she says, reaching into a metal cabinet in the corner of the room. "There are other emergency supplies in here, too. We'll need everything. Help me."

Elias and I race to fill our pockets and packs with the stun guns, medical supplies, bottles of water, and other emergency gear.

"We'll need Lacy close," Emma says. "It's the only way we can hack her with Bellaton's terminal."

"You sure you know what you're doing?" I ask.

Emma sighs. "That terminal is top-of-the-line, much better than what we used for Talen. I'll use it to tap into her programming. She might become unstable, but I'll do my best."

Once Lacy realizes what's happened, will she have the strength to forgive herself, or will she lose her mind?

"I'll get her," Elias says. In a flash, he moves to the door.

"And Bellaton and Reinhart," Emma says. "She won't come alone. It will look suspicious."

Elias nods. He swings open the door and rushes out.

Emma and I get set up at Bellaton's desk. She preps the inputs and hardware connected to the computer terminal for tapping into Lacy's nanites.

My body tightens with each movement. *Free Lacy. Escape unharmed. Destroy the EHC.* The stab of a headache forms at my temples.

A few minutes later, Elias brings all three back inside the office. Scowls and frustration fill each of their faces. Lacy clenches her fists and her eyes narrow on me again.

"What did you say to the SNA?" Bellaton demands.

Reinhart pulls from Elias' grip. "Answer her."

"Nothing," I say. "We haven't made a decision on your future yet."

Bellaton raises a brow

"What do you know about the no-fly zone?" Emma asks, shifting her eyes between Bellaton and Reinhart.

Reinhart moves toward her. "Why would I answer you?"

Even with Elias' weapon trained on her, Lacy's hands begin to rise. I pull my gun around and hold it at my hip and she lowers them. The odds are not in her favor.

Bellaton pushes past Reinhart. "The lockdowns were established well before our time. We were told under strict orders to never break the protocol. Tampering with it leaves the city vulnerable. You have no authority to change that."

Lacy stretches her fingers and tilts her head from side to side. My heart picks up the pace as she does it.

"Control her!" Elias shouts to Reinhart.

Inching forward and unafraid, Lacy raises her hand to Elias' neck.

"Move!" I yell, and Elias darts to the side.

I reach into my pocket with my free hand and pull out one of the stun weapons, zapping Lacy with it. She falls to the ground with a *thud*.

"Tie her up," I order Reinhart. "Lacy's service to you is over. I'm bringing my friend back."

CHAPTER 16

REINHART'S EYES FLASH with anger. "How dare you!" he growls and lunges, swiping wide with his hand to pull me down.

"Fin!" Elias shouts.

I step back just as Elias raises his gun and clocks Reinhart's head with a crack, knocking him out and sending the commander crumbling to the ground.

Bellaton rears back. "What have you done?"

"The same thing I'm going to do to you if you don't comply," Elias says.

Bellaton presses against the wall and runs both hands through her hair.

Taking a deep breath, I wipe my forehead and refocus on Lacy. "Give me Reinhart's belt."

Elias quickly pulls it through the loops and hands it to me.

Lowering down to Lacy's side, I tie the belt tight around her hands.

"Will that hold her?" Elias asks.

"It'll have to do. It'll at least give us a few seconds." But I remember how dangerous Talen was when we tried to deprogram him.

"She'll be deprogrammed faster," Emma says, fiddling with a pair of repurposed medical sensors. "We may not need as much restraint. If I can just get to the nanites—"

"You'll never break through," Bellaton mumbles.

Elias jabs the gun into her side. "Stay quiet!"

Bellaton narrows her eyes at him and then shifts her gaze outside the window, probably trying to will a heroic rescue of herself with her mind.

Lacy's head turns from side-to-side, and she groans as if she's fighting through something.

I chew on my lip. "She's coming around. How much longer?"

"The protocols," Emma says, tapping away on Bellaton's terminal, "they're buried deep. It's not as easy to break in."

"Of course not," Bellaton says. "You're in the Command Center. Did you think we'd just hand everything over to you?"

"No," Emma says, "but I've just accessed the command codes for opening the no-fly zone."

Bellaton's jaw tightens.

Emma swipes past several more pages of data. "They weren't hard to find."

"You've got to hurry," Elias says.

Beads of sweat drip down my cheeks and my heart pounds in my chest. I squeeze Lacy's hand. "Hold on," I whisper.

"She doesn't stand a chance," Bellaton says.

My nostrils flare and I stand. If we didn't need the director so badly, I'd march over to her and shoot her dead. A slow grin spreads across Bellaton's face. I'm sure she knows how important she is.

Suddenly, a red beam flashes into the room, drifting toward the back of Emma's head. My gaze follows it to the window and then to the op on the rooftop next door and a nearly hidden gunman. He peers over the top of a sniper rifle before returning his gaze to the scope.

"Get down!" I yell, dropping to my knees.

Emma dives to the side of the desk. The sniper's bullet pierces the thick window, shattering it into a million pieces. Elias slides behind the wall, pressing himself flat next to Bellaton, securing her with his gun to her head as I shield Lacy.

"You've got to lock down the building!" Elias shouts to Emma.

She reaches up and pulls the terminal down to the ground. Shielded by Bellaton's desk, Emma continues to work on breaking through the protocols.

Elias raises the comm device and presses the button. "If you try to take us out," he shouts into it, "I'll kill Bellaton—don't test me!"

Warm air mixes with the cool air conditioning. Voices from outside mingle with several shouts from the street below. I squeeze my eyes shut and try to take long, slow breaths. I swallow, hoping to stay calm.

"Can you keep them out?" I ask Emma.

"I'm trying." Her fingers move quickly. Each swipe on the screen brings up more information, jumbled pieces of code, and more data. Emma's eyes flash as if she's deciphering everything just as fast as it comes up.

Sliding back to Lacy's side, I feel for her pulse. It pounds in her wrists and a vein in her neck pops out as she moans in agony.

A heavy *thud* comes from just outside the window. Turning, I jump back as a metal panel locks in place, covering the opening.

"There," Emma says, straightening back up. "The building is secure." She exhales a sharp breath. "Now for Lacy."

Elias rushes to the door. "I need to check on the others—watch Bellaton!" he yells.

I shift my gun from my side and aim it toward her head. Bellaton stiffens.

"You don't have to point that thing at me," she says. She lowers down to her heels. "If I'm dead, so are you."

My breath hitches. "Move closer to the door," I order her.

Her eyes strain and flit around the room, but she complies, stepping over Reinhart, then leaning against the wall.

"You don't know what you're doing," Bellaton warns. "You're going to get everyone hurt or killed. Why don't you leave now? Take my hovercraft—it's on the underground level. You can get away, and I'll make sure no one pursues."

I shake my head and tighten my grip on my gun as my stomach churns. A second later, Elias returns. "Sky, Drape, and Talen are still on guard out there. They say we're surrounded by ops— twice as many as before."

"The SNA is our only option," I say. "We have to ask Morris to meet us—"

"You're making a huge mistake!" Bellaton interrupts.

Elias turns a cold gaze toward her. "Shut up with your lies."

"Can't we move Bellaton back with the others?" I ask.

"No," Elias sighs. "We might need her to give us access if Emma can't break through."

"And what makes you think I'd do that?" Bellaton says.

In one swift move, Elias cocks his gun and holds it to the side of her head. "We're way past niceties now. This is going to work, or both our worlds end today. Are you willing to go there?"

Bellaton's body stiffens. She clenches her fists and lowers her gaze.

"I've got it," Emma says. She hands several wires to me. "Connect the sensors."

I take them and place the pads on Lacy's temples. Her breathing picks up.

"I can hack into her nanites and reprogram her," Emma says, "but you need to listen very carefully. Once I break through, she may become agitated."

"I know," I say and check the security of the belt around her wrists. "We've got it."

"Let's do this," Elias says.

Emma swipes her fingers on the screen and Lacy arches her back and groans.

"Come on," I whisper to her.

Sweat streams down Lacy's forehead. She twists harder and kicks, nearly knocking me back against the wall.

"Hold her!" Elias shouts.

"I'm trying," I say, gripping tighter. "It's okay." I lean closer to Lacy, gripping onto her shoulders as tears burn at my eyes. "You're going to be okay. Keep fighting. You're almost out."

But instead of being okay, her eyes bulge in pure agony and tears stream down her cheeks. Jagged red lines fill the whites of her eyes. Her mouth hangs open as if her jaw is locked in a permanent, silent scream. Then, without warning, her body goes into convulsions.

"Come on… come on," Elias says.

"She's almost through," Emma says. "A few more nanite pathways and we'll have them all."

I wrap my arms around her to hold her steady. Just as quickly as the violent shudders came on, they end, and she collapses into my arms.

"She's got a regular pulse," I say as I lower her to the ground.

"You've ruined her," Bellaton says.

"No." Emma narrows her eyes. "*You* did that."

Lacy's eyelids flutter open. "W-what happened?" she asks in a weak voice.

My breath catches. It's been too long since I heard the real Lacy. "They forced the Aura modifications on you," I say, "but everything is okay now."

She pulls herself up. Her eyes search mine and fill with tears.

"Don't," I say to her. "You don't need to say anything right now. You just need to rest. We'll find a way to work through the other stuff later."

"I don't feel right," she says and slumps to the floor.

"We'll need to move her to a more secure location soon," Emma says.

"Where?" I ask.

"The whole building is secure for now, so we have time to try the SNA again."

Elias reaches for the comm and tosses it to Emma.

She clicks through to the secure channel. "Ambassador Morris?"

It only takes a few seconds and the device pops to life. *"I'm here,"* he says. *"Is everything ok?"*

I take a deep breath and lean closer to the comm. "We had to do something," I say, not wanting to spend another minute inside the EHC headquarters.

Emma nods. "We'll agree to meet with you outside of the Ethos city limits."

"We'll need the no-fly zone open to get to you," Morris says.

I turn my attention to Elias. "What choice do we have?"

Elias sighs. He takes the device and says, "We'll open a small section of the no-fly defensive perimeter."

"No, no, no," Bellaton groans.

I glance at her, sitting against the wall. Her hands twitch as she shakes her head back and forth. "You cannot do that." Leaning her head back against the wall, Bellaton presses her lips together, and then says, "You'll get us all killed."

My head fills with all the EHC's lies. Everything that comes from Bellaton's mouth feels like another layer of deceit.

"Do it," I tell Emma.

While Emma arranges the meeting point with Morris and opens the no-fly zone, I check on Lacy. Her breath is still shallow.

Elias moves toward the door. "Let's get Lacy into the hall."

Together, we slide a mostly unconscious Lacy toward the door and into the hallway. Once there, we prop her up against the wall.

"I'll get the others," Elias says as he runs to the office next door.

I glance at my friend again, not wanting to leave her, but return to Bellaton, who's staring toward the blocked-out window. Beside her, Emma finishes up on the terminal.

"It's done. The passage is clear. The perimeter is open."

A part of me wonders if Bellaton feels as trapped as I've felt for my whole life. I shake off the feelings and take a deep breath, sensing how close we are to finally being free.

"Let's go," I say, ordering Bellaton to her feet.

"Just let me go..."

I laugh. "No way. You're our bargaining chip, remember?"

She turns her head to face me. "What does it matter? No matter where you go now, we're all going to get killed."

"Not if you're with us." I point my gun at her. "In the hall."

Emma and I head toward the door, past a still unconscious Reinhart. Bellaton walks toward Sky, who secures her against the wall outside the office.

Beside Sky stands Drape, wide-eyed as he stares down at Lacy.

I place a hand on Drape's shoulder. "Don't worry, okay?"

He swallows. "Is she—?"

"Deprogrammed?" Emma asks. "Yes."

Sky reaches down to Lacy, but Drape pulls back, a sudden look of fear turning his face pale. "Keep her away from me," he says.

"She's not like she was," I assure him.

"I don't care," Drape argues. "She *could* be. You don't know. I just want to get out of here."

My shoulders drop as I realize how long it will take to heal the deep wounds of this war.

"What's the plan to get out of here?" Talen asks.

I look around at the group. No one speaks. "Why don't we split up? If one of our groups gets caught, at least we'll have the other to bail us out."

"You should lead Sky, Drape, and Emma to the meetup point with Morris outside of Ethos," Elias says to me. "We'll meet you there once everything is set up. Bellaton will stay with us just in case the EHC tries anything."

"I'll stay here with you, too," Talen says. "With Lacy." His eyes go to hers and he crouches at her side. Lacy leans against the wall, now more alert and blinking back tears. "I know what you're going through," Talen says to her.

If she's anything like the Lacy I remember before the enhancement, she'll fight with all the strength in her body to get back to who she is. There's no one as strong as she is. Strong, bull-headed, determined, and with my help, there'll be no stopping her.

"Are we going to head out on foot?" Drape asks.

"No," I say, remembering the hovercraft underground. "We can take Bellaton's personal transport hovercraft."

The director cringes at my words.

I snatch Bellaton's badge from her jacket and turn to Elias, pointing at the comm device. "Keep the line open."

"I will," he says, a wry smile on his face.

Taking a deep breath, I try to form the words, but it's impossible. We've been through so much, and there isn't time to say everything I want to.

As if sensing my conflict, Elias reaches out a hand and takes mine. "Be safe," he whispers.

"I will," I say, squeezing his hand, then letting go to wave for the others to follow. "Let's get out of here."

As Sky, Drape, Emma, and I head out of the Command Center, we rush past a cracked-open window. Below us, dozens of ops line the street. We're surrounded, but with Bellaton still secured with Elias, Lacy, and Talen, no one dares take another shot.

We make it to the elevator, and the doors open for us to rush inside. Breathless, I flash Bellaton's badge to the security scan and press the underground level button. The elevator's slow humming makes my stomach swirl. I grip my gun, sure there will be hordes of ops as soon as the elevator doors open underground. My pulse throbs through me in fast beats, making me wonder if this whole thing ends with us dying in a shoot-out, only now in an elevator instead of Bellaton's office.

I hold my breath as the elevator stops and the doors slide open, then relax once I realize we're really in the underground lot with no ops in sight.

"Which one?" Drape asks as we scan the dozens of sleek-looking transport machines.

"There," I say, pointing to the black hovercraft parked a few yards away. It screams privilege and must be Bellaton's. We rush to it, pull open the doors, and climb in.

"Do you think you can fly it?" I ask Emma.

She raises a brow. "I just broke into the EHC command codes, reprogrammed Lacy, and opened a thirty-year-old no-fly zone. I think I can fly a hover."

I grin as she has us up and off the ground in seconds. The engine roars to life, and the slow humming of the blades push us up and out past the security checkpoint into the dawn rising over the horizon beyond the EHC headquarters.

Exhaling a deliberate breath, I gaze at the beauty of the city. Every building sparkles in majestic black. As we climb higher, there's a sense of freedom that soars through me.

"Look at that," Sky says, gesturing outside the window.

I follow his arm. Below us, ops line the street. There are dozens and dozens of them, all waiting for their opportunity to destroy us. All they need is the command, but they'll never get it.

I lean back against the soft cushion of the hovercraft. We've finally made it.

CHAPTER 17

IN A MATTER of minutes, we're flying out of the city and into the remote outskirts of Ethos. My eyes are glued to the changing landscape; the roads widen, buildings shorten and then disappear until the only thing left is open patches of dry earth surrounded by the bones of empty buildings long since forgotten.

"How much longer?" I ask Emma.

"We're almost there," she says as she maneuvers toward what looks like an old factory surrounded by boulders and a few dead trees. The outer bounds of Ethos feels like a wasteland of used parts. Heaps of metal and crumbling towers mark where once there was a thriving civilization, long before the changes to the world, but now they stand as only a reminder of what once was. I take a long breath.

My heart skips a beat as the steady humming of the hovercraft slows and Emma lowers the craft to the ground.

"Where's Morris?" Sky asks as he peers out the side and front windows. "You said he'd be waiting for us."

Emma scans the landscape. "We have no idea how far away he is."

The air from the blades kicks up the dirt surrounding us. A cloud of red soil blows gently in the wind not twenty feet away. Emma disengages the engine and opens the door. A blast of warm air hits my face, followed by particles of dirt that cling to my lips and hair.

"I'm not going out there," Drape says, folding his arms across his chest.

Reaching back, I grab hold of his arm and pull him from the hovercraft. "We're *so close* to ending this," I say to him. "Aren't you excited?"

"No." He pulls away. "I've had enough of negotiating and fighting. I'm tired."

"We all are," Sky says.

I cough and wipe the dust from my eyes. Around the hover is nothing but desolation for miles, reminding me of our journey to Mason's training camp.

"Let's wait for Morris over there," Emma suggests, pointing to an area beside the factory, a small clearing with shade from the sun.

"Come on," I say to Drape. I pull out a bottle of water and hand it to him. He takes it with a sigh, then follows.

Once we've reached the clearing, I take a seat on a giant boulder. I crack open a bottle of water for Sky, then open one for myself while Emma takes a long, slow drink from hers. Electricity pricks at my skin. Finally, we're free of the EHC.

I bump shoulders with Drape. He frowns and kicks a small rock across the ground. "What's taking them so long?"

Sky scans the surrounding area. "They'll be here."

I adjust the strap of my gun. The air is dry and hot. I want to be excited—this is a new beginning, a chance at a normal life—but thoughts of Lacy still won't quite let me. To shake off my nervous energy, I tap on the end of my gun.

Emma digs through her bag and pulls out the comm. "I'll try to make contact with them again." She tries to tune the channel, but there's no response other than crackles. "The signal is weak due to those tall structures around us," she says. "I'm going to move closer to the hovercraft."

"I'll go with you," Drape says, following her.

Sky returns to my side. "She'll be all right."

"Who?" I ask, taking another drink.

"Lacy," he says. "I know you're worried about her."

"Aren't you?"

"She's better now than when she was as an Aura op."

I nod, knowing she's just starting on the path to healing herself. "She's been through a lot."

Sky turns his gaze back toward Ethos. "And we haven't?"

Leaning back, I take a deep breath. Exhaustion pulls on every muscle in my body. That, and the adrenaline I've been running on is starting to ebb. "When this war is finally over, we'll all have to come to terms with our choices."

"Lacy will," Sky says. "No one blames her."

My gaze drifts to Drape, standing by Emma's side. "He does."

"Drape will be all right. Give him time."

"We'd better see what's taking them so long," I say, moving from the rock toward Emma. Sky follows.

"So?" Sky asks when we get there.

"Nothing," Emma says. "But they're probably making sure the no-fly zone has really been lifted."

I tug on the strap of my gun. Drape paces, then eventually sits on a hunk of building and drops his head into his hands while his foot taps on the ground. Just then, the comm device crackles, and he's up and back by my side.

Emma holds up the device. "Hello?"

"Emma?" Elias says. *"Are you there?"*

My shoulders drop. I grab the device from her. "We're here. Are you safe?"

"We're still secure," he says, *"but the ops are swarming the place outside. How much longer?"*

"I don't know," I say. "There's no sign of the SNA yet." My eyes flit from Sky to Drape. "How's Lacy?"

"She's fine. She's coming around."

"Good," Emma says. "Keep her moving and talking. It will help her to reestablish a familiar sense of herself once she reconnects."

"Will do."

Drape turns his gaze back toward Ethos. He walks as if he's heading back to the city. I hand the comm back to Emma. "Keep trying to make contact," I say, then head after Drape.

"Where are you going?" I shout.

He stops and turns to face me. "They're not coming. I know how this works. You get your hopes up, everything seems to be working out, and then it fails. It's basically like our entire life."

"I have to believe things are changing, and for the better."

"How do you know?" he asks.

"We've disrupted the EHC's system. That's enough. They're no longer an isolated power."

Sighing, Drape leans against the fallen part of a brick wall.

I lean beside him. "We've managed to infiltrate and cripple a system that was impenetrable."

Drape turns his gaze to me. "None of this would've happened without you."

"And you," I say.

"I admire you," he mumbles. "No one is as brave as you. I would've given up a long time ago."

"That's not true," I say, heat flooding my cheeks. "You're braver than you think."

A slow smile spreads across Drape's face, a light rekindling in his eyes.

"Once this is over, we'll get back to our normal lives."

"Normal?" Drape echoes. "I hope not. Normal in the mines was not so great."

I chuckle. He's totally right. We have no idea what normal is.

Drape turns to face the city again. "A new life, a home, friends, and—"

"Never having to answer to the EHC," I finish.

He turns back to me and his face brightens.

"Hey!" Sky calls out to us from the hover.

I turn to see him pointing at something in the air. Shielding my eyes, I spot what looks like hovercrafts—a dozen of them, maybe more. My heart swells. Turning back to face Drape, I say, "They're here."

We race back to Emma and Sky.

A few seconds later, the hovercrafts get close enough for me to see their grey and black exteriors. Medium ships lead while larger ones trail behind. I wave a hand to them. Drape, Sky, and Emma do the same. My head tingles with excitement.

"Where are they going to land?" Drape calls to Emma.

Emma stops smiling as she stares hard at the sky. "They're not."

Her words hit me hard. "What?" I say, facing her.

"They're flying too fast. They're going past us," she says.

As I return my gaze to the armada, I feel the blood drain from my face. Emma's right. They're not slowing down. "Maybe they don't see us."

"They see us." Emma steps back to the hovercraft. I shift to grab Drape's hand, but he's too fast as he rushes back with Emma.

"I don't get it..." Sky says.

"They're flying toward Ethos," I say, chasing after Emma and Drape.

"Get in," Emma calls, waving Drape inside. I grab Emma's shoulder before she has a chance to board the hover.

"Why aren't they meeting us? "

Her face is lined. "Get inside and stop asking questions."

Shaking my head, I turn in time to see a bright white light followed by a *boom* in the distance. The ground shivers under my feet.

"No!" Drape shouts, holding his hands to his ears.

"Are they *bombing* the city?" Sky asks in disbelief. "There has to be a mistake. There has to be—"

"It's *not* a mistake!" Emma yells. "The SNA betrayed us. They *used* us. Now get inside!"

More *pops* in the distance echo and fire erupts out of the city. I try to force my feet to move, but my body is stiff with shock. My thoughts scatter between freedom and disaster. I swallow and run my hands through my hair as I imagine Elias, Lacy, and Talen fighting for their lives as the bombs continue to drop.

More flashes of light are followed by clouds of black smoke and loud explosions. My eyes stay glued to one of the collapsing towers as one of the SNA's largest hovercraft steers away from the wreckage.

"Fin!" Emma yells. Her voice feels hollow, like an echo. "You need to move!"

Slowly, I turn and get in, leaning back against the seat as the door closes. All of my words to Drape just moments ago were empty. Lies. I slam the back of my head against the cushion of the chair and scream in frustration, then lower my head to my hands. Hot tears rush to my eyes and stream down my cheeks. When I finally look up, Sky and Drape stare blankly ahead while Emma grips the controls, her knuckles white and her eyes fixed. She pushes the control all the way down. The hovercraft shakes as it picks up speed.

"We have to get back to the headquarters," she mutters. "Fast. Maybe they haven't bombed it yet."

Every ounce of hope inside of me wishes the same, but I know if I were to attack the EHC, it would be the first building I'd drop a bomb on. Emma's eyes are locked forward, as if she knows the same.

"We're going too fast," Sky says as the sides of our craft begin to rattle.

"Put on the seatbelts," Emma orders.

We quickly strap in.

"I'm sorry," I whisper to Drape, reaching for his hand. He pulls away and leans his head against the window.

As we reenter Ethos, my gaze turns toward the streets. Citizens rush from burning buildings below. Rubble is scattered over the ground. Dead bodies lie in the streets. I press my hands to my temples as panic sears through my veins.

"Watch out!" Sky yells. I look up and see a sleek grey SNA hovercraft pull out of nowhere. It's twice as big as ours, and a missile heads straight toward us.

Emma swerves, but the missile grazes the side of our hovercraft, opening up a gaping hole in the metal at my side and sending us into a vicious tailspin. My body jars left, then right. The belt around my waist snaps. I scream as I feel myself falling out through the hole.

"I've got you!" Drape yells. I feel his hands around me as he pulls me back into the hovercraft. Our eyes meet as wind rips around us. He's at my side, unsecured from his seat. I take a deep breath and squeeze his hand.

"We're going down!" Emma yells. "Brace for impact!"

The streets below rush at us and fear locks me in place when everything goes black.

***

When I open my eyes, nothing surrounds me but fragments from the craft. A buzzing sound in my ears reminds me I'm still alive. My trembling hands trace my arms and legs. Blood covers my body. The taste of metal lingers in my mouth. I try to move, and pain erupts from every part of me, searing through to my core. I cry out as I roll to my side, trying desperately to get to my hands and knees and find my friends. Around me there's yelling. I guess that's what it is, but it sounds like it's coming from a different world.

It can't end like this.

People rush past. Fire burns all around me, and the smell of charred flesh penetrates my senses.

"Fin!" Sky cries. "I need help!"

Pushing past the pain, I force myself up. I turn to follow his voice through black smoke and a haze of fire and ash. As I get closer, I see the hovercraft has broken into two pieces. From the front, Emma slowly emerges from her seat. Blood trickles down her head. She coughs and points to Sky, who's wedged into the second piece of the machine.

"Get me out," he says.

Black spots form in front of my eyes and mix with the blood that continues to run down my forehead. "Hold on," I yell as I try to get closer, climbing between the wreckage and pieces of a building that collapsed nearby. Somehow, I manage to see into the hovercraft and glance down at Sky's legs, which are wedged tight behind one of the seats. I scan the area for something to use to get him out of there.

"I'll be right back," I say.

"Where are you going?" Sky demands.

Limping toward the back of the hovercraft, I look around. There has to be something I can use, but all I can see is panic and destruction and my mind won't settle for long enough for me to figure it out.

The screams of an injured woman lying in the street pierce through the fog in my head. My eyes land on the bodies all around me, twisted and destroyed. Many more are hurt and lie on the sidewalk. They reach desperate hands to me, begging for help.

"I can't," I say. "I have to help my friends. I have to—"

My gaze falls on a familiar face lying half-twisted and bloody in the nearby rubble. I shake my head as I try to erase the image. When nothing works, I climb over the debris toward it, half-believing it can't be, but by the time I'm there, I know it's real. There's no taking back what's done.

"Drape!" I yell, ripping the rubble from his limp body. "He's not breathing!" I scream at everyone and no one, clawing at the debris around him, tearing metal back with all my modified strength.

CHAPTER 18

I GRIT MY teeth as I pull a massive rock from Drape's legs and heave it to the side. His blood streams from his forehead and his right leg is twisted beneath his body.

"Hold on." My voice shakes as I reach down and feel for his pulse. "Stay with me, Drape."

It takes a while, but finally, I feel a faint vibration. My hands shake as I scan over his unconscious body for injuries. There's a deep gash to the cheek, what looks like a broken femur, and a possible crushed pelvis. Without the right equipment I don't know for sure, but it doesn't look good.

"Help!" I scream, shifting more pieces of debris off him. When it's mostly cleared, I press my hands to his chest and focus on compressions. Desperately, I breathe into Drape's mouth and pump on his chest, forcing oxygen into him and blood to circulate. Resuscitation was one of the first skills we learned underground. Mining is dangerous, and people got hurt all the time.

Muffled bombings in the distance mingle with the sounds of screaming people and collapsing structures.

I have to stay focused. I can't let Drape die. He's my family.

"Come on!" I plead as I try again to breathe life into him.

From behind, Emma yells. I whip my head around to see her and Sky. Emma's eyes are glued on Drape's body. She helps Sky over the rubble toward us and places him not far from us on the ground. The sight of Sky, battered and torn up, brings another layer of guilt to my already aching chest. His pant legs are shredded. A giant cut lines his forehead.

"Hurry! I need your help!" I shout to Emma.

She races to my side.

"W-what do I do?" I stutter.

"Is he breathing?"

My eyes fill with tears. "I... I think I felt a pulse."

She rolls up her sleeves. "Keep working on compressions. We've got to get his heart started."

Without question, I begin again. Kneeling next to Drape's limp and twisted body, Emma examines him from head to toe before leaning back on her heels.

"He's too far gone."

"No way," I argue. "Drape's a survivor. Look at how far he came." The words come out between sobs.

Emma runs her hand through her hair. "His body is too weak from the impact. He must have been thrown out from the hover. There's nothing—"

"*I* was thrown out, too. If I can survive, he can."

Another nearby blast nearly knocks me to the ground. The heavy smell of burning fuel fills my nostrils as several small EHC hovercrafts collide midair. The sound of shattering glass hitting the pavement is followed by more screams.

"We can't stay here too long," Emma says. "It's too dangerous out in the open like this."

"I'm not leaving Drape."

"Let him go," she says, slowly standing.

"What?" Her words slip past me and my heartbeat pounds in my ears. "He still has a pulse! He's not gone!"

Just then, Drape's eyelids twitch and flutter open.

Between a gasp and cry, I stop compressions and reach down for Drape's hand, pressing the other to my chest.

He smiles at me.

"Stay with me," I order him. "I'm going to get you help, but you've got to fight, okay?"

A trickle of blood leaks from the side of his mouth. "If I knew I'd have to die to get your lips on mine, I would've done it a long time ago."

I brush away tears and laugh. "Just hang on, okay?"

"How bad is it?" he whispers. "I c-can't feel anything."

"Don't worry about that," I say. "We'll fix it. You'll be fine."

Drape gives me a weak smile, as if he knows I'm lying.

I turn to Emma. "Please, there's got to be something—maybe if we move him."

"Where? The city is collapsing. Nowhere is safe right now."

I scan in every direction and my chest tightens. Smoke billows from broken buildings. The SNA hovercrafts dart around the sky, blasting any EHC defense away. Another bomb drops in the distance.

Emma's right. I choke back a cough and try to swallow, but my throat is dry and sore from inhaling the toxic fumes. I press my fingers to my temples, fighting back the urge to scream as Emma digs the comm out of her bag.

"Is he going to be okay?" Sky asks, limping over toward us.

When I glance back, Drape's eyes are still. "No!" I yell, feeling his neck for a pulse.

"He's gone," Emma says.

Refusing to listen, I start compressions again. My hands work fast as I move from his chest to his mouth and back again, willing life into my friend. My arms ache as I pump down on his motionless body.

"Fin, please," Sky says. "He's gone."

I know it's over, but if I stop, then I'll have to accept it, and I can't. I can't give up on Drape, not when he never gave up on me. I'm alive right now because of him.

"Please stop," Sky says. I feel his arms wrap around my waist and he pulls me to my feet. Just as fast, a wave of despair blankets me.

When Sky lets go, I stand staring at Drape's pale face. His whole body is limp and broken. They're right… he's gone. No one can bring him back now. I scramble to his side and brush his hair back from his face. Again, tears flood my eyes. I lean over and kiss his forehead, a wave of regret washing over me.

Sky's hand on my shoulder brings me back to reality—to the bombs that drop around us and the collapsing buildings.

"Fin, I'm sorry."

His voice barely reaches my ears. I slowly turn and fall into his arms and cry.

"You did all you could," he whispers.

"I could've done more," I say, pulling back as a surge of anger consumes me. "I should never have gotten him into this situation."

"These things happen in war," Emma says, stepping closer.

Clenching my fists, I rip myself from Sky's embrace. "It was obvious. Everything was too easy. The SNA was too willing to help. We should have known."

"We were lied to," Emma says. "We had to take the chance."

Another enemy. More lies. A world full of deceit. My stomach churns as I realize Bellaton and Reinhart were telling us the truth. I flex my fingers and hold back the urge to punch something. The very people I'd grown to hate and distrust were telling us the truth. Or, at least, a small part of the truth, although it was only to save themselves, not us.

"And look what happened," I say, pointing back to Drape. My chest tightens as I realize Drape's devotion to me got him killed. "He would never have followed us if not for me. He was tired of war. He wanted to leave the fighting, end it—"

Another blast shakes the ground. The tremors rumble up my legs and rattle my teeth. After a moment, the roar of another building collapsing subsides.

"That was near the EHC headquarters," Emma urges.

Sky leans over, looking straight into my eyes. "There's still time to help the others."

Emma tries the comm again. Still no signal. Only the familiar crackling static. "We have to go there to help the others."

"How?" I check the quickly changing landscape. "The streets are full of wreckage."

"We'll have to figure it out," Emma says.

I pull back my shoulders. If there's a chance to rescue them, we have to take it. I glance back to Drape's body. "I can't leave him."

Sky raises a brow. "He's dead. There's nothing more we can do—"

"No. I'm not going anywhere until I know his body is secure."

Emma glances at Sky, then holsters the comm. "I'll help you lift him back to the hovercraft."

Renewed energy from my already healing body mixes with my determination to do everything I can to make up for what I failed to do when Drape was living. His body was too far gone to heal, even with his modification.

Together, Sky and I work to rush Drape's body from the rubble and toward what's left of the hover.

"In the back," I say.

Once Emma opens up the door, we slowly lower Drape inside. I kiss my fingers and press them to Drape's head, saying one last goodbye, then close the door.

"Okay," I mutter. "Let's go."

When I turn, Emma has the comm ready in her hand again. She presses the side and lifts it into the air, trying to get a signal. "Elias, come in."

All that returns is static.

I check the gun still strapped to my side as we move toward the street.

"Stay alert," Emma says, looking up at the buildings flanking us. "No telling who has eyes on us right now."

I take a long, slow breath as we race through Ethos. Only hours before, the majestic black buildings shimmered. Now, a dull coating of dust and sand coats the remaining windows that haven't been busted out. Citizens rush past us. A few moments later, several ops emerge from a building. I hold up my gun ready for battle, but they run past us.

"It must be bad if the ops are abandoning their posts," Sky says.

I force my feet to move faster, climbing over another pile of smoking metal and cement, around more dead bodies, past holograms permanently stuck in a gyrating flicker.

"The EHC headquarters are there," Emma says.

"How do you know?" Sky asks. "Everything looks the same now."

"The ops," she says, pointing to a group of guards who struggle to pull Reinhart from the partially collapsed structure.

I blow out a sharp breath and follow Emma and Sky to what's left of the building. "Where are they?" I yell at the ops, but they ignore me.

Reinhart moans. The guards help him to sit up.

"They're not going to help us," Sky says.

"They don't have to," Emma says. "I found them."

I follow her gaze to the side of the street where Lacy sits along what was once a sidewalk. Standing beside her are Elias and Talen. They're badly cut up, but they're alive.

My pulse speeds up. It feels as if I'm getting another chance to make this right. I rush to them and throw my arms around Elias.

"You're alive," I say.

"We made it out just before the building collapsed." He pulls back and winces. Burns cover his forearms and hands. "The front entrance was bombed," he says when he sees me looking. "But Talen got it the worst."

My eyes flash to Talen. A deep cut penetrates the back of his head. He teeters on his feet, as if he might fall any moment.

Emma puts pressure on it stemming the blood flow. "It should heal in a few minutes," she says, helping him to the ground.

"What about you?" Elias searches my eyes.

I gulp back the words, then finally manage to get out, "I'm fine. There was a crash. The hovercraft—it was hit by a missile. I've mostly healed, but…"

As if slowly registering the situation, Elias' eyes bounce from face to face. "Where's Drape?"

It takes me a few seconds. Finally, I lift my chin. "He didn't make it."

"Drape's dead?" Lacy says as she stands and faces me. The look in her brown eyes is human again, full of life and the same regret I feel. Her face flushes as she shakes her head.

"We did everything we could," Sky says. "He was too injured."

Lacy wraps her arms around her waist. "I-I can't believe it."

"No one can," I say.

"But, I… I *did* this!" Lacy cries. "I got you involved. If it wasn't for me, he'd be alive."

My breath hitches. Before she can say another word, I hug her tight. "It's not your fault," I whisper.

An SNA hovercraft swoops close. Too close.

I pull back. "They're not going to stop until the command center is destroyed."

"We need to go then," Elias says. "Get out of the city."

"Can Talen walk?" I ask Emma.

Talen nods. "I'm fine. Nearly healed."

I take a long look at each person in our group. We're all healing from the attack and getting stronger, but each of us carries a battle-weary stare, and beneath that the fresh wound of another loss.

"We should go underground," Emma says. "It might be the safest place."

Panic at the thought wells inside me. "No way," I say.

Emma takes a long look around. "If we stay here, another bomb is going to drop on us, or one of the EHC guards will take us out."

"But we have..." I scan the group for Bellaton. "Wait, where is she?"

"Dead," Talen says. "Crushed in the falling debris."

I hitch back my shoulders and secure my gun to my hip. "We need to protect ourselves from the EHC ops," I say. "They'll be looking for revenge." My gaze turns to Reinhart, who's slowly coming around. One of his guards hands him a bottle of water and helps him to his feet. "We have to take him."

Elias turns a concerned eye toward me as another bomb falls nearby. The loud *boom* rattles me to my core, but I push past it and go with Emma and Talen to pull Reinhart to his feet. Sky and Lacy work to force the guards back.

"After all you've done," Reinhart hisses. "You've destroyed Ethos and compromised the EHC's thirty years of peace and order—"

"You can blame us later," Elias says. "Right now, we've got to get somewhere safe."

Reinhart narrows his eyes. "Nowhere will be safe for you now."

"Then apparently we have the same problem," I say to him, waving the others to follow.

Elias moves to the front of the pack and leads us back into the belly of Ethos. The deafening explosions tear into my thoughts, forcing me not to think, and for that I'm grateful.

CHAPTER 19

"Where are you taking us?" I ask Elias.

"There's an underground hovercraft port up ahead," he says between breaths.

I grip my gun and my eyes shift from rooftops to alleys, sure we're going to get attacked by an EHC op or bombed by the SNA.

"What happened back there?" Elias asks.

"We waited," I say. "Then the SNA hovercrafts flew right past us. They were headed straight for the EHC headquarters."

Elias grits his teeth as he swivels toward an op who rushes past. Sky and Talen cut him off, but the op puts his hands up and rushes away. Behind him, a hail of gunfire erupts from approaching SNA operatives on foot. Nearly a dozen charge at us, all wearing dark green uniforms with silver trim and black helmets. At least they're dressed differently than the EHC.

"Move!" Emma yells as we rush to avoid getting hit.

Reinhart groans as we drag him away. One of his ops flies back from a barrage of gunfire. With a *thud*, his lifeless body now lies in a pool of expanding blood.

I duck for cover and breathe deeply to try to slow my pounding heart. It doesn't work.

"That was close," Lacy says. "Too close."

"You don't even know who you're fighting anymore, do you?" Reinhart says, dusting off his jacket. "Or how *to* fight them."

"Stay quiet," Elias orders.

"You opened the gates to the SNA," Reinhart growls. "We'll all be dead soon if you keep letting them kill my guards."

Around the corner, several more SNA ops gather. Sky waves for us to follow him to an alley and we creep into the narrow passageway. Talen forces Reinhart ahead of him and against the wall.

"The entrance to the hovercraft port isn't far," Elias says. "We just need to wait until the guards move and then make a run for it."

The enemy ops fan out, blocking our escape, but getting underground is our only chance to survive the non-stop bombing.

"Why don't we take them out?" I ask.

"Too many," Elias says. "Besides, I'm low on ammo."

Sweat drips down my cheeks. I brush it away and check my gun. It's the same for me, only a few bullets left. One more battle might spell disaster. It would be nice to have a rechargeable blaster right about now.

Beside me, Lacy holds her hand to her head, probably struggling with the reprogramming. Her ability could neutralize the SNA forces, but she's not fully recovered yet.

"You okay?" I ask.

She leans back and presses her head against the brick wall. "It's all coming back," she says. "I didn't want it to come to this."

Reinhart turns a cold eye to her. "You *begged* for us to enhance you."

"No… no, I didn't," she insists.

A chill rushes up my spine as I imagine what she must have seen under Reinhart's authority. Too much death, no doubt.

"Just hold on," I tell her. "As soon as we're out of this nightmare, things will get better."

She laughs as if that's the best joke she's heard all day.

All around us is the smell of death and smoke, and my throat tightens. I need to get out of this tight space. I glance down to the end of the alley, where debris litters the ground. A soft wind blows bits of ash around the sky, and a wall of crumbling rock keeps us from heading through and around to the other side.

"You're like a bunch of scared rats," Reinhart chides. "Hiding in an alley instead of fighting."

Emma pushes between us and to Reinhart's side. Her stern eyes tell me she's had just about enough fighting for one day. She presses her hand against Reinhart's shoulder, forcing him into the wall. "I'd stay quiet if I were you."

"Or what?" he asks. "You'll need me to make it out of here, which is highly unlikely."

"We need you," she says, "but not necessarily in one piece."

Reinhart tries to shift away, but beneath her firm hand, he stays put.

"Now," she says. "What do you know about the SNA?"

"Stories," he says. "I've heard nothing but stories about them. Several outside groups have wanted to infiltrate the EHC. We get threats every day. What do you think we've been doing for the last thirty years?"

"Your way of controlling only benefited *you*," I say.

The commander turns his gaze to me. "You don't even know what you're talking about. Without the EHC, you would have been dead a long time ago."

"You don't know that," I say.

"There have been past attacks on the outskirts," he says. "Skirmishes. But no one made it to Ethos or any of our other cities. Not until now."

"Ethos is destroyed because of *you*," Emma hisses. "One word back at the headquarters would've changed everything. We would never have agreed to—"

"We *warned* you—" Reinhart starts to yell.

"No," Elias interrupts, backing Emma up. "You didn't tell us everything." He holds his gun to Reinhart's chin. "But now you will. What are we up against?"

The veins in Reinhart's neck pulse. "I didn't know it would be the SNA," he says, twisting away. "It was classified information. Kept away from everyone—even me. This world is a big place and we have many enemies."

My eyes flash to Elias. I doubt Reinhart's telling the truth, but if he is—

Reinhart rubs at his chin as Elias pulls his gun back. "The perimeter was closed. It was to protect *all* of us."

The thought of something worse than the EHC makes me shudder. Protected *by* the EHC feels like a joke, but I never imagined there could be anything worse than them.

"There must be something we can do," Sky says. "We have to be able to keep them from gaining control of Ethos."

"You really messed up," Reinhart says. His eyes narrow at Elias. "It was stupid to open the no-fly zone." He runs a hand through his hair. "You think you know so much and you don't."

Behind me, Lacy lets out a low growl, and I spin around. Her hands are clenched, and a darkness covers her face as she raises her fingers to Reinhart. Suddenly, Reinhart drops to his knees and claws at his throat. His face turns red as he gags.

"S-stop her," he sputters.

"Lacy!" Talen shouts, pulling her back. Released, Reinhart slumps forward.

Nothing gives me more pleasure than seeing Reinhart struggle, but Lacy's use of her Aura power is a step in the wrong direction. "You can't do that," I tell her.

Her dark eyes soften. "After everything he did—"

"Focus on healing yourself," I say. "Killing him now only makes you like them."

She swallows and nods.

Emma crouches next to Reinhart's limp body. "He's out," she reports.

"At least it shuts him up," Elias mutters.

Sky pokes his head around the corner again. "We've got to move. No sign of the SNA fighters."

Elias holsters his gun, bends down, and heaves Reinhart's body over his shoulder. With the path to the hovercraft port open, we race down the street, around more debris, fires, and wreckage. It's only two city blocks away, but every step feels like it might be my last.

Our feet pound the pavement, each of us running as fast as our tired bodies can move until we reach the opening of the barely-standing building and slip inside, then follow the stairs down into a subterranean parking lot where half a dozen hovercrafts are parked, untouched by the bombing. The cool air inside envelops my body. I take a deep breath of the smoke-free air.

"Put him over there," Emma says to Elias, pointing to a wall.

He lowers Reinhart against the post, then moves fast to the first hovercraft, one of the larger ones, and smashes the side window with the butt of his gun. "We can take this one," he says, pulling the door open.

Sky and Talen climb in and help lift Reinhart to one of the back seats as Emma and Elias work to break through the security protocols.

I pull Lacy to the side. "What was that back there?"

She taps her legs with both hands and nervously bounces from foot to foot. "Reinhart said I wanted this. I didn't."

"Of course not," I agree.

"I wish I didn't remember what I did to Drape, but I do. I remember hurting him. I loved that little guy—"

"He's forgiven you." My throat tightens with each of my words. I rub my hands together. "That's the kind of kid he was."

Lacy presses her lips together. Her smile is reassuring and reminds me of how things used to be. "Listen…" she reaches out for my hand, "you have to believe me. When the EHC came for me, I didn't *want* to be turned into an Aura op."

There was a time when I would've second-guessed her, but not now. "Even if you wanted the enhancement," I say, "I know you would've never wanted to hurt Drape or anyone else in our group."

"I didn't," she says. "But I couldn't fight it. Every part of my brain told me I had to hurt him. I had to kill. I had to destroy. I had to—"

"It's all over," I assure her.

"I tried to stop Reinhart," she says, glancing to Elias and Emma. "Do you think they'll believe me?"

"In time."

Her shoulders drop as she turns her gaze to the ground.

"I'm just happy you're back," I say, squeezing her hand.

Suddenly, the hovercraft charges to life. Elias waves for us to get in. "We have to leave," he says. "No telling when the SNA will drop another bomb, especially if they figure out this is a hovercraft port."

Emma steps closer to Lacy, examining her face. "Do you remember your life underground?"

"Of course," she says. "It sucked, and they made us work like slaves."

Smiling, Emma pats Lacy's shoulder and says, "She's all right. Almost back to her normal self. Memory recall is one of the last things to return."

But I know her full recovery is a long way off, and doubt she'll ever return one hundred percent to who she was before the enhancement.

None of us will ever be the same.

"Let's go," I say, grabbing Lacy's hand and heading toward the hovercraft. We climb in and Sky closes the door. Ahead of us, the metal wall shifts open, letting in the outside light. It floods the port and splashes across our faces. Dark circles cling beneath our eyes.

Emma and Elias click buttons along the dash and secure their belts. "Hold on," Elias says as he turns to me. "It's going to be a challenge getting out of here."

Talen leans closer to Lacy. "If you need anything—"

She nods and whispers, "I might." The whole experience has definitely taken some of the edge out of her.

As the hovercraft moves forward to the edge of the opening, two SNA crafts zip past. My breath hitches as Elias pushes the craft forward, and seconds later we cruise out into the air. Red and black mingle in the sky as if the sand and smoke have merged, creating a haze that blocks out the sun.

In the front, Emma tinkers with the comm, flipping through channels until, finally, the crackling static fades. "I think I've found something."

A moment later, Ambassador Morris' voice comes through loud and clear, shouting out orders to his soldiers. My eyes go wide. A dozen things that I want to say to him go through my head.

"We're connected into the SNA's main channel," Emma says as she lifts the device to her mouth. "Ambassador Morris," she yells.

The shouting on the other end goes quiet. Sky and Talen lean in just as Elias snatches the device from Emma's hand.

"How could you do this to us?" he shouts. "You betrayed our trust. What you did is nothing short of pure evil!"

Again, there's silence. The hovercraft makes a sharp right turn to avoid an SNA craft. Up ahead is the edge of Ethos and its burned out buildings.

"Ah," Morris says. *"You're still alive. I thought you'd be killed or chased off a while ago."*

"You don't know us very well," Elias says.

"And you don't know us, either," Morris says flatly.

"How could you do it?" Elias demands.

Morris laughs. *"It is not my fault you chose to believe me."*

My blood begins to boil, and I shift my gaze out the window.

"You do have one thing to look forward to," Morris says.

"What's that?" Elias asks.

"You will be remembered as the group that brought the EHC to its knees; the beginning of their end. You assisted in the rise of the Sovereign Nerics Alliance. Soon, we'll have full control of Earth."

I unbuckle and lean forward. "We don't want a part in your plan!" I shout.

Reinhart's eyes begin to open. He shifts his head left and right, then focuses on us. "Where are we?"

"Getting out of here," I say.

Emma takes the device. "So that was your plan," she says. "All along you've just wanted to control the Earth. Take the power from the EHC and eliminate anyone who got in your way."

Morris clicks back. *"With the Enhanced Human Coalition gone, no one can stop our purification of the planet. Only those willing to dedicate their lives to the SNA can exist. When the rotation of the magnetic poles is complete, the planet will be reborn to those worthy of it."*

My stomach churns. His familiar tone reminds me of the EHC's smug superiority.

"You're just another version of the EHC," Elias says, as if in tune with my thoughts.

Reinhart straightens himself. "Cut communication," he orders.

Emma ignores him. "How are you different from the EHC?"

"It's nothing about wealth or status," Morris replies. *"It's about those who honor the chosen and dedicate their lives to the coming new world."*

It feels the same to me. Whether fighting for money, status, or honor, someone is going to suffer.

The hovercraft shifts left to avoid a missile spinning in circles toward us.

"We're nearly there," Elias says.

I glance behind us at Ethos, nothing but a black, burning city. Structures collapse beneath plumes of dust and smoke. Slowly, I turn back, forcing myself to look ahead.

"Ambassador Morris, you *must* call off your attack!" Emma shouts. There's no response. "He's gone," she says, dropping the hand that holds the comm into her lap.

"What are we going to do?" I ask. "They've already decided the fate of everyone here and within EHC territory."

Reinhart shifts up in his seat. "Apparently, we now have a common enemy. Not that I want to work with common Slags and defectors—"

My chest tightens as I realize what he's saying. "How can we stop them?"

Reinhart leans forward. "There's a covert comm channel connecting the EHC and Aura Op units. With access, I can mobilize a sizable army to take on the SNA."

I chew on my lip. My eyes flash to each of my friends. There's so few of us left to take on another fight.

The hovercraft clears out of the city and into the desert.

"Hand Reinhart the comm," I say to Emma. "He's joining our band of rats."

SCORCHED: CHAPTER 1

A month later…

THE COOL AIR hits my face, sending a sudden shiver down my spine. My room is on one of the lowest underground levels, making it extra chilly this early in the morning. The intense heat during the day outside won't warm the place up for several more hours but having most of our operations underground prevents any heat signatures from giving away our location.

"Way too early," a muffled voice sounds.

A smile fills my face as I roll over and curl up into Sky's warm arms. "We have responsibilities you know."

Sky wraps his arm around my waist, pulling me closer to his core. "Five minutes, please."

"Fine, but if Emma needs you for another scouting run, you better be ready. I'm not taking the blame this time."

"Yes ma'am."

These last few weeks with Sky have been amazing. Even with the world crumbling around us, I have someone to go to each night—someone to remind me there can be something better.

My eyes become heavy, but an intense pounding on the metal door jolts me awake. Two more thuds echo through our small quarters.

"Give me a second!" I shout to the door.

I swing my legs over the edge of the bed, and goosebumps instantly cover every inch of exposed skin. My body tightens as I quickly throw on a fresh pair of dark jeans and a tank top. I almost grab Sky's sweatshirt and pull it over my head but decide against it because it will just be too hot up top. Instead I wad it up and chuck it as Sky's head. Bullseye.

"Hey," he mumbles, rustling in the bed, but instead of getting up, he only pulls the blanket over his head, letting the sweatshirt fall to the floor.

I let out a scoff that he doesn't respond to and walk over to the small sink and mirror in the corner of the room. My reflection makes me do a double take. The dark bags under my eyes and wild hair circling my head makes me cringe. I splash water on my face and reach for the small towel hanging off the sink, drying away the fatigue. It's time to do something about this mess of hair. I grab the brush on a small shelf next to the mirror. The knots are tough to work through, but I grit my teeth and manage to tear them out. When I'm done I pull my hair into a simple ponytail and head toward the door.

Unlocking the latch, I swing the heavy door in and take a few steps out. Elias, along with a couple of the EHC ops under his command, leans up against the back wall to the side of our room in a common area. Elias avoids my gaze, keeping his head down and his arms folded.

"What is it?" I ask, looking back and forth at them.

Elias straightens and finally looks at me. "Reinhart is having Talen, Lacy, and the rest of the Aura ops take out a check point near the perimeter breach. He and Emma thought it would be smart if we take a team and give them support."

It still digs at me that Reinhart is giving orders, but he has the fighters and tactical insight on his side. At least, Emma is shadowing him at Command. We're one big happy family I guess.

"I'm going with you," Sky says, shirtless and leaning up against the door frame.

Elias rolls his eyes. "Whatever, but we need to head out in an hour, meeting in twenty."

Ever since Sky and I have been together, Elias has been pulling away from me. I know Elias and I have a connection, but I didn't know how strong his feelings for me were. Maybe I did, but it's not fair that he's been shutting us out the last couple of weeks.

Elias orders his team down the hall. I turn to Sky and shrug. "What was that?"

"What?" He returns the shrug.

"You know very well what I'm talking about. Give Elias a break; he has a lot on his plate and he doesn't need you rubbing us in his face."

Sky heads back into the room. "He needs to get over it."

"Just behave on this mission, ok?"

"I will, I promise," Sky says as he gets dressed.

A minute later, we head out of our room and down the corridor. We need something to eat. Heading toward the mess hall, we pass the rec area where several of the former Dwellers from my underground mine are sitting and playing games. Us Dwellers are used to being up early for our shifts, so it doesn't surprise me to see so many people up and about. While this bunker takes up nearly half this mountain side, we are getting pretty packed in here ever since we liberated the Dwellers that were hiding in the Slack.

"Sky!" A young voice calls from behind us.

Turning, I see Cia run and jump into Sky's arms. Their mother trails close behind Cia with a warm smile lighting up the room.

"Hey sis, how'd you sleep?" Sky asks Cia, and then reaches out to embrace his mother.

"Pretty good," Cia says to him. "They moved in an extra cot, so mom and I don't have to share a bed anymore."

"That's great."

Since Sky and I have been together, I've been getting closer to his family and it's been nice. It's something I've never known outside of my connection with Drape and Lacy.

Sadness washes over me. Drape would've loved this place. Sure, we are still at war and fighting for our lives, but there is a sense of unity and freedom that we never had underground.

Out of the corner of my eye, I see Lacy and Talen enter the mess hall laughing. Turning, I catch Lacy playfully jab him in his side. They've bonded over their Aura connection. Lacy has really changed since we've been here. It's like she has a sense of purpose now. She makes eye contact with me and nods before turning her eyes down and smiling. She turned eighteen last week and has been using that as motivation for a new start in life. I guess Talen might be part of that new start—at least for now. Lacy's never been a relationship type of girl.

I gesture to Sky that I am going to grab some food. He smiles and turns back to his mother.

As I head to the food table, a tall EHC op bumps into me hard. "Oh, sorry Slag, I didn't see you."

"You better be careful who you bump into," I snarl.

"Or what, you'll open another section of the no-fly perimeter and let more enemies in to kill us?"

Not everyone is a fan of this new arrangement, but so far there haven't been too many incidents between our people and the EHC. But there are occasional flare ups.

"Just stay out of my way," I say.

"Will do, Slag."

I grit my teeth and my right-hand forms a fist. I'm just about to let it meet this jerk's face when a hand catches my upper arm and pulls me away from him.

"This is where you got away to," Sky says to me through his teeth.

My nostrils flare, and I twist back to the op who's already gone.

"You should have let me punch him," I say.

Sky shakes his head. "Save it for the real people we need to fight. Let's get our breakfast."

Breakfast consists of some bland oatmeal and reconstituted powdered eggs. No fruit today. The meal's not great but no worse than anything I had in the mines, so I get two bowls and an extra helping of eggs, and then proceed to work on the meal at a table far away from my new nemesis.

About halfway through my second bowl of watery oats, I check the time and realize we're going to be late to meet up with Reinhart.

"We need to get moving," I say to Sky and scarf down the last of my food.

Sky shovels in the rest of his food while he stands. When he's done, the two of us make our way to headquarters, but not before I throw a scowl to the op I wanted to give a beating to a few moments ago.

"Take a rest, my little warrior." Sky smirks as he pulls me through the exit.

I punch him in the arm, and he rubs it as if I really hurt him.

"You better toughen up if you're going to be with me," I tease and sprint ahead of him.

Sky chases me down the hall, and I laugh as he tries to catch me. The two of us race up the stairs a couple of floors with him still in my dust. I exit on the floor with our destination and, finally, Sky catches me in the hall. I let out a laugh.

He spins me around and plants a kiss on my lips, and for a tiny second, I melt into his arms, forgetting all the crap around us.

"Mm-hum," a female clears her throat.

My eyelids flick open, and I see Emma standing against the door frame of the headquarters room, her eyebrow raised.

Sky and I jump back from each other, and instinctively I straighten my shirt and cross my arms over my chest.

"Sorry, Emma," I say.

She chuckles, and her eyes twinkle a bit. "Get inside." She gestures inside the room and turns to enter it.

Sky stifles a laugh and leans into me. "We'll continue that later," he whispers in my ear.

Heat rushes up my chest and neck at his words, and I slip my hand into his.

Apparently, everyone is on time but us because inside the room waits not only Emma and Reinhart but Lacy, Talen, Elias a handful of EHC ops and a female Aura with dark skin and a short pixie cut. Reinhart is dressed in camo and works at a computer display with the others over his shoulder.

"This is the location we are targeting." Reinhart points to a large map on the display. "It's an SNA checkpoint near the outskirts of Ethos."

Emma waves us over. "The SNA has still not been able to open the perimeter fully, so only a few ships can get in at one time. They've lost the element of surprise, and the entry point is heavily guarded. But in time they will most likely be able to open a larger section. We need to keep that from happening."

"So, what is it you need us to do?" I ask.

Reinhart turns to us. "If you were here on time you might have known the answer to that question."

My lips form a thin line, but I don't look away from him.

"You'll need to weaken any efforts by the SNA to take Ethos and get access to the EHC network fully," he finally says. "They don't have Aura tech, and it's time to take advantage of that fact." He looks to Lacy and Talen.

Talen nods. "Understood, sir."

Sky and I return to our quarters and gather a few supplies as well as check our weapons. We don't say much. There's nervous energy bouncing from the walls.

"You ready?" Sky asks, holstering his pistol.

I nod. "I have to be."

We make our way deep inside the mountain fortress to the north side where the others wait. There's a bustling of activity inside the large hanger. Thick, riveted, metal walls reach up at least thirty feet high. Near the hanger doors everyone from the meeting except Emma and Reinhart sits silently in a medium-sized hover with Talen piloting.

I've caught Elias glancing over at Sky and me at least twice. No matter how many times I remind myself I have nothing to be ashamed about in my relationship with Sky, I still get a pit in my stomach when he looks at us.

"Location ahead," Talen says from the pilot chair. "Ready your weapons."

I place my hand on the pistol on my lap and pick it up. With a sigh, I check the weapon and lay it back down. I stretch up from my seat to get a view out the front window. In the distance, a hard-hit and charred compound is set on the horizon. A fleet of SNA ships patrol in the air and there are countless soldiers on the ground that look like extremely well-organized ants below. We're heading straight for an SNA army and we are heavily outgunned. If we get any closer, we're dead.

To Be Continued

∞

Exclusive Updates as well as free content: Be the first to find the latest on the Manipulated series as well as Harper's other work. In addition, get free content, giveaway opportunities, and other exclusive bonuses by joining my VIP List at **www.harpernorth.com**.

Thank you for reading Ascended, book three in the Manipulated series. If you enjoyed reading this book, please remember to leave a review on Amazon. Positive reviews are the best way to thank an author for writing a book you loved. When a book has a lot of reviews, Amazon will show that book to more potential readers. The review does not have to be long—one or two sentences are just fine! I read all my reviews and appreciate each one of them!

www.harpernorth.com

Acknowledgements:
Special thanks to Torment Publishing! Without you this book would not have happened. I love you guys.
Thanks to all the early beta readers and the support of my fans.
Thanks to all my family for the support!

Credits:
Chase Night - Editor
Jack Llartin - Editor
David R. Bernstein - Publishing & Marketing Support
Jenetta Penner - Publishing & Marketing Support

Made in the USA
Middletown, DE
23 November 2018